For Tommye

THE WIDOW'S WOODS

Mignon F. Ballard

Carroll & Graf Publishers, Inc.
New York

Copyright © 1991 by Mignon F. Ballard
All rights reserved

First Carroll & Graf edition 1991

Carroll & Graf Publishers, Inc.
260 Fifth Avenue
New York, NY 10001

Library of Congress Cataloging-in-Publication Data

Ballard, Mignon Franklin.
    The widow's woods / by Mignon F. Ballard.
    — 1st Carroll & Graf ed.
        p.   cm.
    ISBN 0-88184-680-5 : $18.95
    I. Title.
PS3552.A466W5   1991
813'.54—dc20   91-4502
                                                  CIP

Manufactured in the United States of America

THE WIDOW'S WOODS

Also by Mignon F. Ballard

Raven Rock
Cry at Dusk
Deadly Promise

For Younger Readers

Aunt Matilda's Ghost

Chapter One

Sometime after midnight I heard the humming. It was that mournful old hymn—the one they sang at funerals: "Rock of Ages, cleft for me." If I'd had a rock I would have thrown it, but I didn't have a rock. All I had was a pillow, and a hot, wadded-up pillow at that. I plopped it over to its cool side and stared wide-eyed at the ceiling.

It felt strange being home again after almost a year away, and I'd have to get used to staying here alone. I had promised my parents I would look after the house and the shop while they took a long-delayed vacation in England. Long-delayed because of me, because I had dreaded coming home.

"You'd be surprised how quickly people forget," my mother assured me. "Everybody has problems, Jane. We can't dwell on them forever!"

Not my problems, I wanted to tell her. Not my hurt: that cold, dull aching that started anew whenever I saw an ad for a bridal dress or happened to glance at the wedding announcements. I could almost hear them tut-tutting, the good people of Sweetsprings: "Poor Jane Cannon! What a shame! Fiancé just changed his mind, they say, backed out on her altogether, and they'd been going together since high school!"

My face felt hot with the memory of it . . . *on Saturday, the seventh of June, at five o'clock in the afternoon* the invitations had read. We would be celebrating our first wedding anniversary by now, maybe even have a baby on the way—although I doubted it. Every time I'd brought up the subject of children, Mac had suddenly decided to talk about his work at the hospital or elaborate on the plot of a movie he'd seen. And now, if rumors were true, he was going to marry someone else. Bonnie Lynne somebody-or-other, who was an anchor woman for a television station in Charleston and looked as if she weighed about eighty pounds and ironed her hair with a steamroller!

I sighed, flopped over, and plodded into the bathroom for a drink of water. The creaking old house that had always been my home should have been comforting to me, but I felt oddly uneasy. I had arrived late, tired from a four-hour drive, and fallen into bed without even bothering to unpack. The place smelled close and musty, although my parents had only been gone a few days.

Sipping the water, I stared out the small back window at the dark woods looming behind us and wondered if the tales my grandfather told were true. The Widow's Woods, he called them, and dreadful things were supposed to have happened there. At that moment I was inclined to believe him. Only a few months before a young girl had been murdered there in what looked like a ritual sacrifice, and the police didn't seem to be any closer to finding out who had done it. Etta Lucas had grown up in Sweetsprings; she sang in her church choir, led the high school cheering squad. Now her strong voice was forever silent, her bright head crushed. Why? Had Etta gone there to meet someone, or was she a random victim? Her death had churned the town into a state of fear and horror. No one in Sweetsprings wanted to admit Etta's killer could be one of them, that it might happen again. There are some things you don't say out loud. But you think them.

It didn't surprise me that the murder had taken place in

the Widow's Woods. I had never liked the woods. As a child they had reminded me of a beard—a giant's beard, foul and impenetrable, spreading over the hills above town. I shivered. Someday the whole village of Sweetsprings would wake up trapped beneath a web so thick the sun couldn't find it.

It was dark; nothing moved outside, and I could barely see the black hulk of the house next door. Whoever had been humming was now quiet. I drank the rest of my tepid water and went back to bed. I was home now for better or worse. (Why, oh *why* did I think of those particular words?) And it was just for one short summer; after all, I had to face people sometime. Still, it was almost dawn before I went back to sleep.

I guess that's why I dozed off in the back porch hammock the next afternoon. I had eaten a late breakfast after sleeping half the morning and spent the rest of the time making a mental list of things to do, people to call. So far I'd done nothing and called no one.

The smell woke me. Something was burning, and it seemed to be coming from the house next door! I swung my feet to the floor and followed my nose across the backyard and through the thick boxwood hedge to our neighbor's kitchen. Inside, dark curls of smoke escaped from a pan on the stove.

"Chloe!" I didn't wait for an answer but pushed open the screen and snatched the smoking pan from the burner. Green beans, blackened and shriveled, stuck to the bottom of the pot. A small black skillet of corn bread cooled on the back of the stove, and a glass of tea, diluted by dwindling ice cubes, made a puddle on the green Formica counter.

"Chloe!" I yelled again. My neighbor would surely be startled to find me in her kitchen after so long an absence, but where in the world was Chloe Applegate? I poked the charred vegetables with a slotted spoon and scraped the whole mess into the garbage can. Had the woman lost her hearing and her sense of smell as well? The worn linoleum felt cool to my bare feet as I padded into the dim hallway where an array of Chloe's relatives peered down at me from a gallery of photographs. A stern-looking lot, not at all like the woman who lived there, I thought.

Was Chloe Applegate strolling about the neighborhood? Cooling off in the bathtub? Maybe she had slipped on the soap. I jumped at the sudden jangling of the telephone at the foot of the stairs, and when my neighbor didn't appear, picked it up on the fifth ring.

"Chloe?" The caller sounded slightly choked and persecuted, as if she had just survived a tonsillectomy with no anesthetic. Eulonia Moody.

I made a face at the receiver. "No, Eulonia. It's me— Jane Cannon. Chloe must've run out for a minute." I wouldn't tell her about the beans. Eulonia would have the fire truck here within minutes.

"Jane? What are you doing there? I thought—" Eulonia didn't wait for an answer, but rambled on about strawberries. "When Chloe comes back, ask her if she still wants them. I told her I'd stop by the produce stand on my lunch hour even though it is way out of my way." Eulonia cleared her throat. "Of course she clean forgot to give me any—"

"Don't worry, if Chloe doesn't take them, I will . . . and thanks, Eulonia." I quickly hung up the phone. How could Chloe stand being under the same roof with the woman? Of course each had her own apartment, and it was a big old barn of a house, built soon after the turn of the century, my grandfather had said. Still, no walls were thick enough to segregate the annoying woman. I had been about nine when Eulonia bought the house and moved in next door after old Mrs. Crowder died. She was the closest neighbor we had, yet you'd have to think twice before borrowing a cup of sugar from Eulonia Moody.

I listened for sounds of splashing as I started slowly upstairs. "Chloe, it's Jane! Where are you?" Still no one answered, and the long, claw-footed bathtub was dry; its bright-flowered shower curtain pulled back and tied. And Chloe's bedroom was empty. White dotted swiss curtains billowed at the windows; a yellow rose shed a single petal on the bedside table, and the air smelled faintly of exotic lilies.

But where was Chloe?

Not again. Not Chloe! The slight, cold tingle of fear that had awakened inside me suddenly melted when I heard the creaking of the porch swing.

But it wasn't Chloe Applegate who sprawled in the swing. Eulonia's daughter, Shelba Jean, finally acknowledged my tapping at the window and looked up at me beneath dark brows from the porch below. "What're you doing here?" she asked, setting her canned drink on the floor.

I leaned on the windowsill. "Looking for Chloe. Have you seen her?"

The girl shrugged and went back to her letter writing. "Not since early this morning. Woke me up calling for that cat."

"You didn't hear her leave?"

"She might have walked down the road a piece."

"Which way?"

"Toward town, I guess. . . . I don't know."

"Oh, come on, Shelba Jean! What do you mean you don't know? She must've left in a hurry. Her beans were burned black as swamp mud. Couldn't you smell them?"

Shelba Jean Moody carefully licked the envelope and addressed it before replying. "Hey, look, I've been at the mall all morning. There's a sale on, you know. How would I know where Chloe went? I haven't seen her since I got back."

And don't care, either, I thought, turning away. Spoiled, obnoxious brat! As much as I disliked Eulonia, I couldn't help feeling just a little sorry for her for always having to make excuses for Shelba Jean. Only a few weeks before on the night of their high school graduation, the girl and some of her classmates had set fire to a patch of the woods above town. Smoking pot, they said, during some kind of occult ritual. If a passerby hadn't noticed the flames, the whole area might have been

11

wiped out; of course it had been in all the papers. I shook my head as I went downstairs. Let Eulonia explain that one away.

I saw that Chloe had left food and water for her cat, Snoop, on a sheet of newspaper by the back door and I called to the huge gray animal, expecting her to pounce, but Snoop didn't seem to be at home, either. Out catting around somewhere, I supposed.

Outside, Chloe's washing hung in the bright sunshine of a South Carolina June. One daisy-sprigged fitted sheet and matching pillowcase flapped on the line next to an assortment of voluminous garments in varying shades of green. Chloe Applegate was tall and emerald eyed with honest-to-goodness auburn hair which was thick enough and long enough to wear as she pleased. She was probably in her late thirties, but had the kind of complexion that would stay radiant and wrinkle free even when she was ninety-nine. Chloe loved wearing fringed shawls, bright print scarves that flowed, and she packaged herself like a tempting birthday gift, but as far as I knew, the contents remained a mystery.

The rest of the laundry lay in a damp wad in the basket and I hung the bedding on the line to keep it from turning sour in the midday heat. It just wasn't like Chloe to go off leaving wet laundry in the basket, food on the burner.

I walked carefully over the gravel drive between our homes, wishing I'd thought to wear sandals. Should I call someone? Report my neighbor missing? But a little over an hour seemed hardly long enough to notify the police. Again I squelched the small stirring of fear. Chloe was a grown woman. She could take care of herself. Still, in a way, I wished my parents were here; they'd know what to do. My hand trembled the least little bit, and I shoved it into my shorts pocket. I could almost hear my mother's voice: "Jane, honey, you're so nervous, emotional—inclined to blow the smallest thing out of proportion." For a while she had hovered over me like a nagging good conscience, a guardian angel. "I really think it might be a wise idea for you to get some kind of counseling," she suggested. Well, I had put my foot down about that. I had already had one too many doctors in my life, thank you!

Our large kitchen felt cool after being outside, and the house was quiet. I glanced at the paperback I had tossed aside in the hammock, at the breakfast dishes in the sink, and thought again of my mother. Constance Cannon washed each dish as soon as it was soiled, unpacked as quickly as possible after arriving, and would never, never consider lazing in a hammock before the sun went down. But my mother was in Europe for at least six weeks, and what she didn't know wouldn't hurt her.

I filled the sink with water to give the dishes a good soaking and brushed crumbs from the table while keeping an eye on the house next door, but there was still no sign of Chloe. Except for the sound of running water, my house was quiet and still. Too quiet, too still. Through the climbing rose at the window, the sun made lacy patterns on the red tile floor. My mother's bright yellow teakettle sat in its usual place on the stove. This was my home and everything was as it should be. Why did I wish I weren't alone?

When I left for the shop a short while later, I still had not heard from Chloe, and Shelba Jean had abandoned the swing, leaving her soft drink can on the porch floor. A boom box did exactly that from somewhere inside. I decided to walk to town, admiring on my way the bright hollyhocks my mother had planted along the old stone wall that edged the road and the deep green canopy of oaks that shaded the narrow path to town.

We lived on what had once been part of the Kennemore estate and our street was still called Kennemore's Crossing. Eulonia Moody's white frame home had housed the overseer and his family when the place was a working farm, and Miss Baby Kennemore, the last of the clan, now well into her sixties, lived on the other side of us in Twin Towers, the old family home at the top of the hill. Our house had been built in the thirties by one of the Kennemore clan who had since moved away, and had been sold to my father before I was born. It was a beauti-

13

ful area of large shade trees and rolling hills, but it was remote, and as a child I had missed having neighborhood playmates.

Chloe Applegate stayed on my mind during the leisurely walk to town, and I stopped at the drugstore on the corner to see if Eulonia had heard from her. But my neighbor hadn't seen her tenant since morning. "She called to me as I left for work," she said, spraying the counter with glass cleaner, "about those strawberries, you know. But it's been so hectic around here I haven't had a chance to get away. Never even got my lunch break!" Eulonia's low voice took on an even more mournful tone. "Had to make do with a Coke and a package of Nabs, and you know what a mess my digestive system's in."

I nodded slowly. I had certainly been told. Often. Welcome home, Jane . . . and how've you been? So nice to have you back! I told myself. If I waited for Eulonia to say it, I would grow old standing right there between the foot pads and the digestive aids.

Eulonia's dark eyes brightened behind bifocals that also could have used a squirt of cleaner. "You don't suppose something's happened, do you?" An orange speck of cracker had attached itself to the dark hair on her upper lip and it bobbed about as she talked. I watched, fascinated. "I mean, you never know what kind of lunatic is running around out there," Eulonia went on. "Why, when I think of that poor little Lucas girl, it just makes me want to cry!" The crumb finally fell as Eulonia's pale jowls trembled. "Maybe I'd better check on Shelba Jean. She's there alone, you know."

I doubted that. Shelba Jean didn't seem the type to hesitate to take advantage of her mother's absence, and I didn't think she would be alone for long, but I assured my neighbor that her daughter had appeared hale and hearty earlier.

I walked slowly up the steep hill to Cannons' Clothing Store. It was too hot to move any faster, and much too warm for those blasted pantyhose my mother felt it nec-

essary for me to wear to work. I peeled them off behind
the counter as soon as I got inside. The store was empty
except for Alice Boggs, the assistant manager, and one
lingering customer who didn't know me from Adam.

"You won't tell, will you?" I whispered after the man
finally decided on his purchases and left.

Alice laughed. "Your secret's safe with me, but I don't
know about him." She nodded toward the departing customer as the front door clanged shut.

The old store had been in the same building for as long
as I could remember, and I liked its dry, musty smell. I
ran a grateful toe over the smooth, oiled floor. "Umm!
Who cares? Besides, he couldn't see me. Who is he, anyway? Probably not anybody I'll ever be seeing again!"

"I doubt it. I've only seen him a couple of times myself;
must be visiting around here." Alice stooped to replace a
box of athletic socks. "I've missed you, Jane. It's good to
have you back!" She leaned on the counter and looked at
me. "How's the house-sitting? You okay out there?"

I knew what she meant. It was awkward being back in
my parents' house where every room held the sting of
memory: the kitchen where Mac and I had studied together, the long, sunny living room where our parents
announced our engagement, the small alcove that had
held our wedding gifts. It had taken three months to return them all. I squirmed back into my shoes. "So far, so
good," I said and told her about Chloe.

"That is odd," she said. "Maybe she had an emergency
with the cat, had to rush it to the vet. You know how
Chloe is about that animal, calls it her baby! She'd have
forgotten all about those beans."

"But her car's there, Alice. Wouldn't she have taken her
car?"

"Not if Snoop was badly injured—if she had to hold
her. Why don't you give her another call?"

But no one answered at the house next door.

"I wouldn't worry too much about it," Alice said.
"Chloe can be unpredictable at times, and you're not used

15

to being out there by yourself. Are you sure you don't want to stay with us a while? What about your grandpa?"

"Papa Sam's on one of his fishing expeditions. Thanks, but I'll make out. I'll have to—at least until graduate school begins in the fall. . . . And Sudie will come if I need her." I turned away to sort through a rack of blouses. Why did everyone treat me like an emotional cripple? I was doing okay on my own.

Alice touched me lightly on the arm. "You'll be fine," she said as if she could read my mind.

I wished I could believe her. Four years after college graduation I was still bouncing from job to job with a degree in art that was worthless, and the few men I had dated recently seemed either self-centered and egotistical or just plain boring. Maybe something was wrong with me.

"You've read too many fairy tales," my friend Sudie once told me. "The dragon ate Prince Charming years ago."

"Yeah, I know," I said. "And Humpty-Dumpty was pushed." Now I was beginning to believe it. I sold sneakers to Hugh Lee Jamison who was in my class in high school and a skirt to Mrs. Chambers in my mother's garden club. Their voices seemed unusually bright, and their smiles wide and welcoming, but their eyes said, "Poor, poor Jane."

I had had second thoughts about giving up even a negligible museum job to spend the summer at home, but Mom and Dad rarely took a vacation, and seldom asked for my help. It was time to let them know they could depend on me. It was also time to shed my paranoia about returning to my home town, and to Mac's.

I was silent as I helped Alice lock up. To hell with Mac McCullough! It was my town, too. I made a face as I slammed the door behind me.

"What in the world was that all about?" Fred O'Leary, editor and sometimes complete staff of *The Sweetsprings Sun,* stood on the sidewalk, mopping his red face with a damp handkerchief.

I laughed. "Nothing that's fit to print.

"And speaking of printing," I added as we walked along together, "have you heard from your columnist recently? I've been looking for Chloe all day."

Fred threw back his head and laughed. "I won't see that one till her copy's due Monday—if then." His face grew serious. "Why? Something wrong?"

"I hope not." I told him about the burning beans. "I've called the house all afternoon—still no answer."

We walked past a display of plastic water toys in the dime store window, and the ugly yellow dress, which Alice said had been marked down for the third time, that was still on sale at Francine's Fashions.

"Oh well, I wouldn't worry about it. Chloe probably remembered something important she had to do and went off without thinking." Fred jammed his hands into his pockets and looked down as he walked. "You'll find her out in that porch swing fanning herself," he told me. "And she'll laugh at you for making such a fuss!" He spoke as if he'd forgotten what had happened to the Lucas girl only a few months before. I hoped he was right.

But Chloe Applegate's side of the house was dark, her dinner still waited on the cold stove, and there was no sign of Snoop. I brought the sun-dried laundry inside and left her a note to call.

Chloe's windows remained unlighted. I took my book upstairs and watched them off and on as I pursued my cunning secret agent through Third World countries and countless pages far into the night.

The next day hikers found Chloe's cat, Snoop, in the deepest part of the Widow's Woods. The animal had been beheaded on what appeared to be some sort of sacrificial altar, and a five-pointed star was drawn in the dust beside it. There was still no sign of Chloe Applegate.

Chapter Two

"**O**h, lord! Chloe's dead! I just know she is!" Sudie Gaines turned from the window where she had been watching the house next door. "It's going to be the same thing all over again. Remember? He did that awful thing to Etta Lucas's little dog. What kind of maniac do we have running around here?"

I didn't know. Didn't want to know. I stared across the darkening yard at Chloe's empty porch swing, the bright geraniums she had planted. Tomorrow Chloe would be there, weeding the borders as usual in her big, floppy straw hat. Tomorrow we would find out it had all been some terrible mistake.

"I'd like to get my hands on whoever did this!" Sudie said with unrestrained outrage. "I'd like to—"

"Come now, calm yourself, Saint Sudie! Don't let me down." Shagg Henry tilted her chin with one hand and made the sign of the cross with the other. "The pope and I have always found you close to perfection, you know."

Sudie said something the pope probably wouldn't approve of and shoved him away with a force that belied her size, but she didn't try to hide her amusement.

I laughed, too. It was almost impossible to be around Shagg Henry without being affected by him. Witty, irreverent, and usually charming, he had entertained our class

19

from kindergarten through the twelfth grade and made life challenging for his parents and teachers alike. I still found it hard to believe he was now a member of the same high school faculty he had tormented only a few years before. I watched him now as he draped his long, agile body over my mother's Queen Anne chair. If I had kept a written record of the times I'd bailed Shagg Henry out of trouble, I'd have an entire library.

Shagg popped a tangerine Lifesaver into his mouth. "Look, I've checked all the doors and windows, but if somebody really wanted to get in, they could. I wish you'd let me stay. I don't like to think of you two out here alone." His friendly face grew solemn. "My God, Jane, if your folks knew what was going on, they'd be back in a shot!"

"Well, they don't know, and you're not going to tell them," I said. "Besides, we aren't sure anything's happened to Chloe at all. She might be perfectly all right."

Shagg just looked at me. "Sure," he said.

Sudie sat cross-legged on the living room floor with her dark head bowed. "I don't even like to think about it," she said. "That poor cat! And why Chloe? Do you suppose she was poking about out there in the Widow's Woods? You know, I heard somebody was thinking of developing that area, selling building lots there. Can you imagine—living in the Widow's Woods? That place gives me the willies. Don't they have any idea where she might be?"

"Not yet," I told her. The police had been all over the place, questioned everybody, even me. Tears burned in the back of my throat. "If I'd just said something sooner, reported Chloe missing, she might be out there now working in the yard."

"Chloe's a grown woman, Jane," Sudie reminded me gently. "You can't be responsible for what someone else does with her time."

Shagg unwrapped another pack of candy and offered it around. He had taken to eating that particular flavor since he gave up smoking, and it made him smell like a Christmas stocking. "Suppose our Chloe had decided to have an overnight romp with a gentleman friend, and you reported her missing? Think how you'd feel then?"

"Better than I do now," I told him. "Besides, I don't think Chloe was seeing anyone special. Mom would've mentioned it."

"Shagg has a one-track mind." Sudie made a face at him.

"Don't you wish old Ralph did?" He leered at her. "Where is lover boy, anyway? When are you two going to tie the knot?"

I saw Sudie warn him with her eyes. He had mentioned the *forbidden* topic—and right in front of poor, vulnerable Jane.

But Shagg appeared not to notice. "Good grief, you've been engaged for over two years," he said, rolling his eyes. "What's the matter, getting cold feet?"

Sudie stuck out her tongue. "He's in Atlanta for a six-week computer course—and we'll marry when we've saved a few bucks and when we're good and ready, thank you." She jumped up and headed for the kitchen. "Any peanut butter?"

I wondered how long they would toss the subject about like a hot potato in my presence. I could imagine us well into our eighties, still edging around the topic. "Whoops! Mustn't mention marriage! Poor old Jane got dumped, you know." Yet it did seem as if Sudie's engagement to Ralph Mitchell had become a permanent status. She had been teaching music at Sweetsprings Junior High for several years, and Ralph had been with his father's accounting firm even longer. What were they saving for, the Taj Mahal?

Sudie returned munching a peanut butter sandwich and licking her fingers between bites. She paused at the window. "You don't suppose Shelba Jean's mixed up in all this, do you? Lord, I'll bet Eulonia's fit to be tied with all this going on over there."

"Eulonia's always fit to be tied," I said. "Especially when she's losing out on rent money. If anything's hap-

21

pened to Chloe, I'll bet she advertises her apartment in the next week's paper."

"I'd miss Chloe's column," Sudie admitted. "It's silly, I know, but I look forward to it every week. How does she know all that stuff?"

Shagg looked from one to the other. "Look, I like Chloe as well as anybody, but you'll have to admit those columns of hers are just a lot of gossip."

Our neighbor's column, "Chloe's-Line," appeared weekly in *The Sun,* and most readers seemed to enjoy it. Papa Sam, my grandfather, claimed it sold more papers than the ads and the front page put together. "I wouldn't know what was going on around here if I didn't read 'Chloe's-Line,' " I said. "What's wrong with it?"

Shagg groaned softly. "Sometimes things are better left unsaid."

Sudie looked out at the street where lightning bugs winked in the dusk. "But the Widow's Woods! Why the Widow's Woods? What's going on in there?"

"And what was Etta Lucas doing there? Remember? They found her in about the same area as Chloe's cat. Why would a girl all alone like that pick such a creepy place to walk her dog? It doesn't make sense!" If I looked out our kitchen window I would see the woods looming black and forbidding behind us. I made fists of my fingers. I had bitten all the nails on my right hand and started on my left.

I used to baby-sit Etta Lucas, and when my mother wrote me of her death back in February I couldn't sleep for thinking about it. She was eighteen and pretty, an only child, and she had been murdered while walking her dog in those woods. Etta's head had been crushed, and blood from her decapitated pet was used to draw a crude five-pointed star on her cheek.

"I never could understand why she chose that place to walk her dog," Sudie said. "It must have been muddy after all that rain we'd been having. Remember, Shagg? I thought we were going to wash away."

22

"Yes, but that was months ago," Shagg reminded us. "Whoever killed Etta Lucas is long gone by now."

"Not necessarily," I said. "What makes you think it wasn't somebody right here in town? Maybe even one of your students? Remember that circle of stones they found on graduation night? Those kids weren't playing drop the handkerchief."

"Those stones weren't even there when that happened to Etta." Shagg fished in his pockets for his keys. He wore faded jeans cut off just above the knees and a tee shirt with the high school logo on it. He hadn't changed much since the days he played football for Sweetsprings High.

"You don't know they weren't there," I said. "From what I've heard the Lucas girl was killed in another part of the woods from where the graduation night fire took place. We don't know how long they've been meeting up there."

Shagg hesitated with one hand on the doorknob. "Jane, whoever did that to Etta wouldn't stay around to get caught. I think our friend Chloe opened up another can of worms and found a snake inside!"

"Lordy, it's hot in here!" Sudie fanned herself with a section of the newspaper. "Isn't the air conditioner working?"

I had just turned the thermostat down and could still feel the sweat on the back of my neck. Maybe it was the humidity. I watched Shagg pull out of the drive and disappear. The house seemed to close in on me, hot, dark, and stifling. "Let's go over and swim in Miss Baby's pool," I said. "The water should be cool by now; at least it's wet."

Miss Baby Kennemore lived in the twin-towered house at the top of the hill and maintained a small swimming pool at the edge of her property adjoining ours. The pool had been there, I think, since Miss Baby was a young girl, and even though I'd never seen her stick one toe in the water, she was generous in allowing our family to swim there.

"Does she still keep that thing up? My gosh, I haven't seen Miss Baby since she retired. You know, they still haven't found a Latin teacher to take her place."

"Mom says she doesn't get out too much anymore," I said. "But then she never was what you'd call gregarious." I started upstairs for a towel. I was already feeling cooler just thinking about it.

"Do you think we should?" Sudie frowned. "I mean with Chloe missing and all?"

"Oh, come on. Chloe's cat was killed up in the woods somewhere. The pool is practically in my own backyard." I paused on the landing. "Stay here and suffer if you want to. I'm going to cool off."

"Okay, but I'll have to borrow a suit."

"Why? Nobody will see us. It's black as pitch over there without the pool lights."

"But suppose somebody comes?"

"Who's going to come? Miss Baby goes to bed with the chickens, and nobody else knows where she keeps the key to the gate."

"But there's that nephew, Dillard what's his name. I don't like his looks in broad open daylight!"

"What nephew?"

"Miss Baby's nephew. He's been staying there a lot; has a part-time job with some construction company, and he's supposed to be taking classes at the community college."

"Well, he must be in class tonight," I said glancing out the window. "It's dark over there. Come on, we used to go skinny-dipping all the time at camp—remember?"

But Sudie shook her head. "That was way off in the boonies somewhere. This is different."

"Chicken!"

Still, I'll have to admit I felt a little uneasy as I stripped off my clothes by the dark poolside. In the grayish glow of Miss Baby's distant yard light I saw Sudie, wearing a borrowed bikini, dive into the other end.

I waded in a little at a time, letting the cooling waters

24

envelop me; then, pushing off from the bottom, I rolled over and floated on my back. It felt every bit as wonderful as I remembered.

"Psst!"

"What?" I got a mouthful of water as I tried to find the source of the whisper. "Where are you?"

Sudie popped up beside me. "Keep your voice down. There's somebody else in here."

"Very funny." I swam in a lazy circle, kicking water in a glistening arc. I felt like a sprite, a mermaid. I could stay here forever, green tinged as a statue, spouting water from my mouth.

Sudie surfaced again. "I'm not kidding! Look over there in the corner. There's somebody by the ladder."

"Okay, you've had your little joke. That's just a beach ball or something." I tried to tread water silently, but all the while I was stroking for the side. Chloe was missing, probably dead, and the Kennemore house was dark, and too far away for anyone to hear me scream. Could a killer be waiting at the far end of the pool?

Water splashed in my face as Sudie pulled herself up on the edge of the pool. "Hurry!" she whispered. "Let's get out of here!"

In the corner by the ladder, something bobbed. Water lapped against the sides, and I felt the chill penetrate my wet body like a cold sword. My knee struck the step in the shallow end as I reached for the hand railing. Heavy water dragged at me, held me back, and a soggy length of filmy cloth circled my ankle like seaweed.

"Sudie, throw me that towel!" I tried to keep my body and my voice as low as possible as I worked to disentangle myself from whatever had wrapped around my foot.

But Sudie's bare feet splashed across the pavement and whisked through the grass. "Forget the towel! *Come on!*" she called. The gate clicked shut behind her.

In the pale glimmer of the yard light I stared at the dripping cloth in my hand. Even wet, the vivid blues and greens of Chloe's silk scarf made it distinctly hers. I tried to fling it from me as I ran for the gate, but it clung to my fingers like a spiderweb. And in the dark pool near the ladder a shadowy figure seemed to move. That was when I began to scream.

Chapter Three

I was conscious of bright lights and voices. A trailing rose tendril scratched a place on my anatomy it had no business scratching. I held the sodden towel in front of me and stared at the small gathering in my backyard. My eyes burned and my throat felt as if I had swallowed a handful of tacks.

Sudie, glassy eyed and pale, pressed against the fence that divided our yard from the Kennemores'; swim goggles dangled from her hand. The rough wood of the garage, still warm from the long day's sun, felt comforting to my bare back.

"Turn around and slip into this. I promise not to look." Someone held up a blue terry cloth robe and I obeyed, sliding my cold, damp arms into baggy sleeves. It was dry and warm, and best of all, large. Gratefully I tied it about me and squeaked a thanks.

"My pleasure." He had a nice smile, nice voice, and a very nice body I noticed, taking in his brown upper torso and sturdy legs. I wanted to stand there looking at him and forget what I had seen in the pool.

Close by someone was crying: high-pitched wails interspersed with sobs. Eulonia. That meant they had found Chloe. "Oh, my God!" the woman screamed. "She was right here all along! Almost in my own backyard."

Eulonia Moody blew her nose into a wad of tissues and snuffled loudly. "Why, it could've been Shelba Jean . . . it could've been me!"

More's the pity, I thought, catching Sudie's eye. Shelba Jean Moody, in black short shorts and a hot pink tank top, hovered behind us like a belligerent little phantom. Miss Baby was there, white-faced and blinking, answering questions to a soft-voiced policeman who had probably been her student, and a man and woman I'd never seen before. We moved aside for a surge of policemen. An ambulance, red light whirling, skidded into the driveway. I shivered and looked away. It was too late now.

"Probably been in there since yesterday. Nobody noticed, I reckon, with all them trees around," the man said matter-of-factly.

"Sash tangled in the ladder, they say. Murder just as sure as I'm standing here." The woman spoke in a knowledgeable whisper. "Poor soul . . . her own mama wouldn't a knowed her."

I stared at them. Who were these people? Where did they come from? I didn't even know them! The man who had loaned me the robe was trying to shoo them away, while Sudie, swathed in what looked like a flowered tablecloth, allowed Miss Baby to lead her inside.

"Dear God in heaven, Jane! Is it true? Was that really Chloe in there?" Florence Gilroy and her plump daughter, Jeanette, hovered over me. The two lived at least three streets away, and in the event of a local catastrophe, were always the first to spread the word. But how could they possibly have known so soon?

Jeanette smushed my hand in her sweaty palm. "Tell me, did you actually *see* her? What was it like?"

I flinched as a warm hand touched my arm and someone held coffee under my nose. It was the same man who had brought me the robe. "Get something hot inside you," he said, "and come away from this sideshow."

I sat at our kitchen table, sipping the strong, hot brew and letting the steam waft into my face. I couldn't seem to get warm, when only a little while ago the house had felt like a steam bath. Sudie sat across from me, the colorful cloth still draped about her, and wept quietly into her hands. Only when Shagg arrived and announced that welcome or not, he was spending the night, did I finally give in and cry.

The widow walked in my dreams that night. A tall, sallow woman, she moved silently, casting a long shadow before her, her face concealed by the hood of a rough brown cloak.

Ma Brumley always wore brown, my grandpa said, and she carried a large wicker basket. It held food, people believed, and hand-me-down clothes for the cast-off children she took in. Years later, the shocked citizens of Sweetsprings learned the truth about the Widow Brumley.

As a child I had loved hearing the scary tales of old Ma Brumley, as only Papa Sam could tell them; and some unthinking parents and nursemaids even used the threat of the legendary widow to control their charges: "You'd better behave or old Ma Brumley'll getcha—put you in that big old basket—and we'll never see you again!"

The Widow Brumley was supposed to have lived in a small cottage in the heavily forested area on the fringes of town that later became known as the Widow's Woods. My grandfather remembered seeing her as a very old woman when he was a small boy. Since she had outlived three husbands and had no one to care for her, the town provided for her in a well-intended but haphazard manner, and when the old woman died, a group of ladies went to the cottage, prepared to do whatever was necessary to put Ma Brumley away.

Papa Sam always paused at this point in the story, and even though I knew what was coming, I would ask, "And then what, Papa Sam? What did they find?"

"Filth mostly," my grandfather answered. "But in a little room at the back of the house, they discovered what looked like a handbook on sorcery—an ancient book of strange symbols and characters nobody could decipher, along with the bones and skulls of animals and a heavy, dark-stained sword.

"And in an overgrown garden behind the house," he went on, "they eventually uncovered the remains of least two of Ma Brumley's husbands and the skeletons of three children."

The story grew more horrible as it passed from one generation to another, until the witch woman was eight feet tall and the tally of the dead reached close to a hundred; and newcomers to Sweetsprings sometimes had the effrontery to doubt the widow's existence at all. But I knew from my own grandfather that old Ma Brumley with her grim basket had once walked the same streets where I had played hopscotch and learned to ride a bike.

"One day I looked up into the old woman's eyes," Papa Sam remembered. "They were yellowish brown and shiny like tiger's eyes, and they looked right through your soul!"

My mother was a skeptic. "The poor old thing was probably just a messy housekeeper who had a Greek cookbook," she'd say. "And maybe she lived next to a forgotten graveyard. How did they know when those people were buried there? And so what if she did have a sword? Why, Daddy, you have one yourself."

Then Papa Sam would turn sort of a purple red and stomp away. My grandpa was proud of the dress sword his great-grandfather had worn in the War between the States and displayed it over the fireplace in his living room. But as far as he was concerned, the widow's evil weapon and his ancestor's honored sword didn't even belong in the same conversation.

I woke with a headache and the residue of nightmares on my mind. I hadn't thought of the Widow Brumley in years until Etta Lucas had been killed in what appeared to be a satanic ritual. And now Chloe! I opened my eyes, then quickly closed them against the morning light. The image of my neighbor's shrouded figure being carried to the ambulance would haunt me for the rest of my life.

How and why did Chloe Applegate end up in Miss Baby's swimming pool while her mutilated pet was found in the nearby woods? The coroner wouldn't comment on how she died; they would have to do an autopsy, he said. Had Chloe been dead when her body was put into the water, or did someone drown her there? Either way I knew it was murder.

The upbeat rhythm of "Penny Lane" with Ringo on the drums blasted from somewhere not too far away. At first I thought Shelba Jean was playing her boom box, but the noise was coming from the other side of the house; besides, it wasn't her kind of music. I stumbled across the hall and slammed shut the window. The owner of the blue robe, who had recently moved into Miss Baby's old carriage house, was washing his vintage Mustang, caressing its bold red sides with a soapy rag in time to the blaring music, and in obvious disregard of Chloe's death.

Sudie moaned and turned over in bed. "What time is it?"

"A little after nine." I headed for the bathroom and aspirin. Each step brought a throb of pain.

"It wasn't a nightmare." Sudie sighed, staring at the ceiling. "It was real."

"Yes."

"What now?"

"I don't know. We wait, I guess, and hope they can piece things together—find out who did it." I fumbled in the medicine cabinet and tapped two aspirin into my hand.

Sudie threw back the covers. "You look as awful as I feel. I thought those policemen would never leave last night."

"Thanks." I made a face in the mirror. "It was almost daylight before I got to sleep, and then that idiot over at the Kennemores' blasted me out of bed with his volume turned up to kill."

Sudie elbowed me aside to brush her teeth. "Shagg still here?"

"The last I saw him he was dead to the world on the

living room sofa," I said, instantly regretting my choice of words. But Shagg's makeshift bed was empty, and a note in his sprawling handwriting stood propped against the sugar bowl. He had left for his summer job at the recreation center, leaving definite instructions (underlined three times) to keep the doors locked and bolted.

I turned the flame on under the kettle and poured milk in a pitcher and put it on the table. Somehow I had to get through this day.

I took my orange juice to the window. "You'd think he'd have the decency to turn down that noise."

"Who?"

"What's his name. That guy who's living in the Kennemores' carriage house—the one with the great body. It's as if he doesn't even care what happened to Chloe."

"He cared enough to loan you his robe. And who do you think called the police? Besides," Sudie added, "if his music hadn't woken us, I might have slept till noon and I have to pick up my car at ten." She stirred coffee in a mug. "Can you drop me by Odell's Garage? I had to get my brakes relined and he closes in less than an hour."

"I didn't know Odell's was open on Saturdays."

Sudie spread marmalade on semiburned toast. "Well, it isn't as a rule, but this new mechanic said he'd work on his own time. He hasn't been there long, and I think he needs the money."

"Does he fix lawn mowers? Dad's is impossible to start, and the grass is already ankle high."

But the garage, I learned later, would not be open until Monday.

"If you'll bring it in by eight, I'll try to have it ready for you before we close," the mechanic promised, wiping his hands on a greasy rag. Nelson Fain was a soft-spoken man with a trim sandy beard; his blue eyes looked serious behind his glasses, but he smiled when Sudie introduced him and apologized for not taking my hand.

I felt myself staring at him as he made out Sudie's receipt. Where had I seen this man before? And when he gave her the keys to her car, their hands touched a bit longer than necessary, I thought. Was I imagining things, or was something going on between Sudie and the shy mechanic?

The house next door seemed deserted when I pulled into our driveway, and I wondered if Eulonia had taken Shelba Jean somewhere out of town until the horror of Chloe's death lessened. I looked at the unpretentious Moody house with its inviting wraparound porch. The stark white exterior was relieved by soft gray trim; rosy geraniums in hanging baskets brightened the entrance; sunny marigolds lined the walks. Eulonia owned the house, but Chloe had planted the flowers, and Chloe had made it home.

Chloe. She was like a bright, bold flower herself. A sunflower. I brought the car to a sudden halt that sent the tires skidding; my hands shook as I slammed the car door, and I sat on the back steps of the house where I grew up and cried for my old friend.

Chloe Applegate had come back to her hometown and moved into the other side of Eulonia's house when I was a junior in high school. She had consoled me with empathy and tea cakes when I missed making the school basketball team and sent me long chatty letters during that first homesick year away at college. She was the one bright spot in our lonely neighborhood, and I was going to miss her. I wiped my eyes on the tail of my shirt. Flowers and tea cakes weren't such a bad way to be remembered.

Intending to take out my anger and frustration on the grass, I dragged the bulky lawn mower from the shed. But the monster machine still refused to start, and after the engine died for the fifth time I addressed it with a few choice words.

"Hey, hold on a minute and I'll give you a hand." The Mustang's owner stood on the other side of the fence in a pair of tan shorts and an even tanner body. He smiled as he came through the gate. I think. I wasn't looking at his face. "Jericho Scott," he said, taking my grimy hand in his. "We met last night . . . sort of."

I worked my way up to his eyes, which were a clear coffee brown. "Jane Cannon, and I think I have a robe that belongs to you. Thanks; it was a rough night."

He nodded. "Must've been a gruesome shock—but murder, though it has no tongue, will speak."

"What?"

He shrugged. *"Hamlet.* You knew her—Chloe Applegate —fairly well, I guess?"

I studied his face before answering. Was he concerned or merely curious? And why was he so sure it was murder? But as Chloe's neighbor, I decided, he had a right to know.

I told him how she had come back to open a nursery school in Sweetsprings after an absence of several years and had rented the other side of the house from Eulonia Moody. "Her father was a Baptist minister here, and she wrote a weekly column for the paper." I sighed. "Everybody knew Chloe, and Chloe knew everybody." I moved into the shade of a persimmon tree. It wasn't noon yet, and I felt hot, cross, and thoroughly grubby. This man hadn't even known Chloe. What did he care? I yawned, but it wasn't because of the company. I told him so.

"Don't guess any of us got much sleep last night," he admitted. "I was glad to see the sun come up—to get out and join the living."

"I know; we heard your stereo," I said with just the slightest measure of irritation.

He smiled. "Ah, yes, the Beatles! Well, why should the devil have all the good tunes?"

Another quote, no doubt. "Have they found out how it happened?" I asked. "I mean, are the police sure Chloe's death was murder?"

"Haven't heard. They seemed to be pretty thorough, but I guess it's too soon to know."

I asked him about Miss Baby's nephew who was supposed to be staying there. So far I hadn't seen a sign of him.

"That would be Dillard Moore," he said, "and he wasn't around last night. Went to Columbia for a couple of days, his aunt says; his mom lives there, you know." Jericho Scott looked down at my lawn mower and gave it a tap with his foot. "Want me to see if I can get this thing started? Sounds like it might be flooded."

I stepped back to give him room. Maybe he would get carried away and mow the entire lawn. I watched from the steps as he flipped over the mower and tinkered with something underneath. He looked up briefly. "You work in that clothing store downtown, don't you? Thought I saw you in there yesterday."

Of course! The departing customer. No wonder he had looked slightly familiar. "I'm filling in until my classes start in the fall," I said, explaining my temporary situation.

Jericho Scott wiped grimy hands on the grass and got to his feet. "So, you're minding the house and the store while your folks are away?"

"Alice Boggs takes care of things at the store. I just help out where I'm needed. And Su—some of my friends are staying here with me at night." I watched as he yanked the starter and brought the engine putting to life. For all his good looks and helpful ways, I knew nothing about this man. I could be standing there with the person who had killed Chloe Applegate.

Chapter Four

"**B**e sure and check on your grandpa's house while he's away," my mom had said, and so I did—being the dutiful daughter that I was trying hard to be. My grandfather had retired from the insurance business after my grandmother died and now spent most of his time doing what he liked best—fishing. Only Papa Sam got paid for it. He and his long-time friend Cooter Edwards hired themselves out as guides to clubs and sporting groups in the area, and he was gone for a good part of the summer. I missed him, especially as I stepped inside the familiar living room of the cottage on I'll Try Street. (When the area was first built, somebody told the developer he would have to think of a name for it, and he said, "I'll try"; but that was as far as he got.) A well-worn copy of Mark Twain's short stories waited on the table by Papa Sam's chair, and the air smelled suspiciously of stale cigar smoke regardless of periodic visits from Ruby Lovejoy who cleaned for him.

There's nothing lonelier than a house that's empty of somebody you care about, so I didn't linger. Mrs. Lovejoy had done her job and the place looked a whole lot neater than mine, yet there was something that wasn't right.

When I reached home, I saw a light burning in the window next door, and I could see Eulonia moving about in the kitchen. As much as I disliked her, I was kind of glad to know she was there. At least Eulonia was familiar. I hadn't made up my mind about the handsome Jericho Scott. And a little germ of suspicion had begun to nibble in my consciousness; it had to do with Chloe Applegate's weekly column.

When Sudie came over later that night I was up to my armpits in back issues of *The Sweetsprings Sun.* "Checking the classified?" she asked, flopping down beside me. "I hear McDonald's is hiring."

"Don't laugh. It may come to that. No, I'm reading some of Chloe's recent columns."

Sudie kicked off one sandal. "Looking for anything special?"

"I don't know what I'm looking for." I read silently, then folded the newspaper and scanned the column again. "This was in last week's. Listen.

"Amo, amas, amat! Is romance in the air?
Perhaps an old flame was rekindled when
a favorite *magistra* attended a college
reunion last week. . . . If I didn't know better,
I'd swear it was Halloween with all the
ghosts about. Am I seeing things, or is
it a masquerade? . . . And speaking of spooks,
what really goes on in the Widow's Woods?
Who meets there in the evil hour? What hidden
secrets does it hold?"

I tossed the paper aside. "The rest of the column's about the Rotary dance."

"What's with all that Latin stuff?" Sudie looked over my shoulder. *"Magistra.* That means teacher, doesn't it?" Her dark eyes widened. "Oh, surely she wasn't talking about *Miss Baby!"* Sudie fell back against the sofa laughing. "Rekindled an old flame! Why, I doubt if the poor thing ever had an ember to glow in the first place!"

I had to agree. Our neighbor had a dull, almost blurred appearance, as if she had been partially erased; even her photograph in the high school annual had seemed vague. "Miss Baby—I know she has an honest-to-goodness name, but I can't remember what it is."

"Lois Virginia," Sudie said, looking again at the column. "It was under her picture in the yearbook, remember? She said she was the youngest of five and the name stuck. Awful, isn't it? But why would Chloe put that silliness in the paper?" She shoved the newspaper aside. "I hate to say it, but sometimes Chloe's teasing could go too far."

"Do you suppose she knew about some kind of sinister intrigue in the Widow's Woods?" I asked. "Like who killed Etta Lucas?"

"Maybe she was talking about what went on graduation night." Sudie shuddered. "Remember how we used to dare each other to go in there?"

I remembered. The Widow's Woods had always held a morbid fascination for me with its gray sunless surface and menacing brown shadows. Even the trees seemed draped in sadness. I felt threatened there.

Sudie yawned. "Probably none of it means anything. I think she made up half that stuff."

"Then why is she dead?"

"What do you mean? Do you think Chloe was killed because of something she wrote?"

"Or something she knew. What else could it be? If anything's really going on in the Widow's Woods, you can bet our friend Chloe knew all about it!"

Sudie waved the column with a flick of her wrist. "Oh, come on! This doesn't sound threatening enough to kill for; besides, Chloe could have fallen into that pool and drowned accidentally."

"Maybe you haven't heard what they found by the pool," I said. "I ran into Junior Dempsey in the grocery store today; he works with the ambulance crew, you know—said they found one of those little star-shaped things with a circle around it spray-painted on the walkway around the pool. It was right over there by the diving board." I stood suddenly and walked to the window. In another hour it would be good and dark. "Maybe the column I'm looking for hasn't been printed yet." I glanced at Sudie over my shoulder. "According to Fred O'Leary, Chloe's next copy wasn't due until Monday."

Sudie slammed both feet to the floor. "No! The answer is no!"

I turned away so she couldn't see my smile. "No, what?"

"Don't pretend with me. I know what you're thinking." She narrowed her eyes at me. "You want to go poking about in a dead woman's apartment looking for . . . what do they call it on 'Perry Mason'? Convicting evidence!"

"And who am I supposed to be convicting?"

"Beats me." Sudie shrugged. "We'll probably never know because we'll end up like Chloe in the swimming pool." She shuddered. "And this time we won't be doing the back stroke."

"But that's where we'll have an advantage," I said. "Chloe couldn't swim a lick. If she died by drowning, all the killer had to do was shove her in over her head."

"Oh." Sudie looked up and frowned. "But, Jane, wouldn't somebody have heard her? Surely she yelled and splashed around a lot. You were here, weren't you? Didn't you hear anything?"

I hadn't, and I didn't want to be reminded of it. Chloe had probably been killed while I enjoyed a leisurely shower or sat down to a late morning meal. The police had asked the same question and I had given them the same answer. On the morning Chloe Applegate died I hadn't heard a thing.

"You don't really want to do this, do you?" Sudie persisted. "How are we supposed to get inside?"

"With a key, of course. I used to feed Snoop and water Chloe's plants when she was away. She kept an extra key under a pot of ivy on the porch; it's probably still there."

"But Eulonia?"

"Eulonia won't know a thing. She keeps that television turned up so loud she wouldn't hear elephants tap-danc-

40

ing on a tin roof! Oh, come on, Sudie. If we wait any longer it'll be too late."

"Is life this boring to you?" Sudie stood reluctantly. "All right, all right! But tell me what we're looking for."

I did, but it seemed as if we would have to stand in line because somebody else obviously had the same idea. In the otherwise dark window of Chloe's upstairs hall someone moved about with a flashlight. "Damn!" I said. "I told you we had to hurry! Now, who could that be?"

"Maybe it's Eulonia or Shelba Jean."

"But why? It's Eulonia's house. If she wants to snoop around Chloe's apartment, she has a right to be there—lights and all! And Shelba Jean took off over an hour ago."

We stood under the pear tree in Eulonia's dark backyard and stared at the window. The dim yellow light faded, then disappeared. "I wonder if he's looking for the same thing we are," I said. "Wish we could get a look at his face."

"I don't." Sudie moved away from me. "I'm going to call the police."

"No, wait! He might get away before they get here, and I want to find out who it is. Whoever's in there will have to come out through Chloe's kitchen or her side door. If you'll hide under that big cedar on the other side, I'll watch the back."

"Do what? You're kidding, aren't you? What if he sees me?"

I gave her the slightest little shove. "Oh, go on! Nobody can see you. And hurry, he might leave at any minute."

"The sooner, the better," Sudie muttered under her breath, but I heard her moving across the lawn.

A mosquito whined near my ear as I waited in the darkness. Somewhere not too far away two dogs held a barking duel, but inside Chloe Applegate's side of the house everything seemed quiet, and the upstairs window was still black. I glanced over my shoulder at Jericho's small apartment half hidden by Miss Baby's apple orchard. Only a dim light burned by the door and his car wasn't there. He must have gone out somewhere. After all, I reminded myself, it was Saturday night and anyone who looked like Jericho Scott would have an active social life.

Briefly the flashlight flicked on again. If I had blinked I would have missed it. Someone was in the small downstairs room Chloe had used as a study. Not much bigger than a closet, the cubicle was cramped between kitchen and bath and contained little more than a desk, chair, and shelves of books on child care that Chloe used as director of the nursery.

If I could move closer to the window maybe I could get a look at his—or her—face. Rather than walk boldly across the open yard, I kept close to the deceiving cover of shrubbery. A crape myrtle limb swept my face, and the sweet smell of the spiraea bush at the corner of the house tickled my nose. Something brushed my ankle and I remembered the iris Chloe had planted there as a border. I heard one snap under my foot. Did that person inside hear it, too?

I hugged the wall of the house and listened. The prowler was either standing still or in stocking feet. I felt around with one foot for the water faucet that protruded from the side of the house, and using it as a step, pulled myself up by the window ledge.

A dark silhouette looked out at me, his face even with my own.

I think I screamed. I must have, because Sudie was instantly beside me. "Are you all right? What happened?"

I picked myself off the dry, hard ground. The study window was dark now, and on the other side of the house a door slammed. "I'm okay," I said. "But hurry, he's getting away. He must have gone out the front."

I heard Sudie swear softly as she stumbled over an oak root, and I carefully avoided doing the same. I ran around the dark side of the house in time to see a figure dart beneath the trees and take off across the yard.

"I told you we should call the police!" Sudie said, panting. "Did you get a look at him?"

"It was too dark and I was too scared." I sank onto

Eulonia's front steps and blew on my scraped wrist. I wasn't going to tell her what I thought I saw—at least not until I was sure.

"What's going on out there? Is that you, Jane? What's all that yelling about?" A puffy-eyed Eulonia, wearing a gaudy orange housecoat and plastic curlers, shuffled outside, then plopped herself in the porch swing as if she meant to guard the door.

"Somebody was in Chloe's side of the house with a flashlight," I told her. "When he saw me, he took off running."

"Where'd he go? Did you see who it was?" Eulonia snatched a dangling curler and stuck it in her pocket. She huddled in one end of the swing and moaned. "It must have been the same man who killed Chloe! Oh lord, what does he want?"

I peered boldly into Chloe's dark window. "Must've been looking for something. Don't you think we'd better see if anything's missing?" I tried to keep the eagerness from my voice. If Eulonia knew how much I wanted to go inside, she'd never let me in.

But Eulonia Moody just sat there, swaying silently. "Looks like none of us is gonna be safe," she muttered into her lap. "I don't know what to do. . . . You reckon he's gone now?"

"I'm sure of it," I said. I felt sorry for Eulonia; I really did. But I knew it wouldn't last.

Chloe's apartment already had that musty, unlived in smell as if its tenant had been gone for weeks. A thin film of dust had settled on the mahogany drop-leaf table in the front hall. Newspapers from the week before were stacked on one end of a sedate Duncan Phyfe sofa, and a dark oil portrait of some remote Applegate ancestor scowled at us from over the mantel. I scowled back. What was it that bothered me? Something about a mantel . . .

"Well," Eulonia said, "it looks okay to me. You sure you saw somebody in here?"

I didn't answer but walked on through to the back of the house. The kitchen still smelled of scorched beans and cat food but remained undisturbed. We found nothing out of order until I switched on the light in Chloe's small office.

Sudie gasped when she saw it. "What a mess! I wonder if he found what he wanted."

I doubted it. There hadn't been time, only time for the intruder to dump a drawer full of papers on the floor and pull folders from the filing cabinet in the corner. A manual typewriter sat on the massive oak desk Chloe had carted home from the army surplus store, but there was no paper in the carriage, and the drawers contained only writing supplies and a few personal letters.

I had my eye on the letters when Eulonia slammed the drawer shut with her knee. "The police will probably want to look at those," she said, shoving us bodily from the room. "Better check upstairs before we call them."

But other than to leave a dresser drawer half closed, the prowler left little evidence in Chloe's bedroom. Her extra house key, we discovered, was gone from its hiding place beneath the pot of ivy; whoever had been prowling about probably had used it to let himself in.

Sudie and I gave our statements—again—to the young policeman who had questioned us the night before. "Are you sure you'll be all right?" he asked after checking both houses from basement to attic. "I don't think that guy's still in the neighborhood, but you might feel safer staying with somebody tonight."

I looked at Sudie who yawned. It was after midnight and we were both too tired to go anywhere else. "We'll double-lock the doors," I promised.

Just before I crawled into bed I glanced once more at the houses on either side. Shelba Jean Moody still had not come home, and neither had Jericho Scott.

Chapter Five

Sometime during the night I woke to rain. Sheet lightning whitened the sky, and thunder shook the timbers of the old house. Lying there, wide awake in the violet-sprigged room that had always been mine, I watched the play of light on the ceiling and suddenly knew what had bothered me at Chloe's and what had been missing at Papa Sam's. Our ancestor's sword was gone from its place above the mantel.

"What's the matter with you?" Sudie asked the next morning at breakfast. "You've been stirring that coffee for the last five minutes."

"Just thinking." I knew if I told her about the missing sword she'd get that silly little Mona Lisa look on her face. Sometimes Sudie can be too practical for her own good. But this time it wasn't just my imagination. With all the grisly goings-on in the neighborhood, I had reasons to be jittery. And frankly, that wasn't the only thing that concerned me.

I watched Sudie spreading peanut butter on toast. "How's your car?" I asked.

"My car?"

"Your brakes. Did that mechanic at Odell's work out okay?"

"Oh. Sure." Sudie concentrated on the toast, smoothing

45

the spread to the edges and rounding off corners with a studied flourish.

"How long has he been working there? Where's he from?"

"Who?" She observed the dregs of orange juice in the bottom of her glass.

"Peter Rabbit!" I waited until she looked at me. "Odell's new mechanic—Nelson what's-his-name."

"How should I know? Besides, what difference does it make?"

I got up to pour more coffee. "For heaven's sake, you don't have to get your dander up. He looked slightly familiar, that's all.

"Hey, you're not leaving?" I stopped in mid step, coffeepot in hand, as Sudie shoved back her chair and put her dishes in the sink.

"It's Sunday, remember? I barely have time to go home and change; and what would the Holly Hills Nursing Home do for a pianist?"

I had almost forgotten that Sudie was the unwilling accompanist for services every Sunday at the convalescent home where her grandmother lived. "If you hate it so much, why do you do it?" I asked.

"Grannie Belle raised me, remember? I owe her that much. Besides, she expects it; I don't like to let her down."

I had never heard my friend say that she loved her grandmother, although she was loyal, even affectionate to the woman who had brought her up. Sudie had gone to live with her grandmother after her parents died in a house fire when she was five, and I remembered her as being much stricter than most of the other parents. Even from a wheelchair, it seemed, Grannie Belle could be rigid and demanding. "Will you be staying here tonight?" I asked, following her to the door.

"Sure, but I might be late. Ralph's going to try to get up for a while and we'll probably go out to dinner somewhere."

"Look, don't worry about it if Ralph wants to stay over," I said. "I'll get Shagg to come."

But Sudie dismissed that with a wave of her hand. "Don't be silly! I'll see you tonight . . . and listen, Jane, be sure and keep your doors locked. We don't know a thing about that guy next door."

And I could say the same thing about your friend the mechanic, I thought, watching her drive away. I was probably making something out of nothing, but I had a sense of uneasiness—almost an emptiness. A light shone from Eulonia's kitchen, but Shelba Jean's shades were drawn. And Jericho Scott's pampered red Mustang was again parked in its usual place. I turned on the radio, but the prowler next door hadn't made the news, nor was there an update on Chloe Applegate's murder.

The house was cool from the rain the night before, and I wandered aimlessly about in shorts and an old shirt. I knew I should return the robe my handsome, tan neighbor had loaned me, but frankly the circumstances embarrassed me and I couldn't think of a tactful way to do it. Besides, he would probably be asleep after his late night out. Later I would launder it and leave it at his door with a brief note of thanks.

I decided this would be as good a time as any to get started on one of the many projects I'd been putting off, so I dragged a bilious green rocking chair from the basement into the backyard and spread newspapers beneath it. I knew I had seen several cans of white spray paint in the storage shed, and I felt my spirits rise as the old wicker chair was magically transformed, along with the grass around it. With a chintz-covered cushion it would look nice in the small off-campus apartment I would be renting in the fall.

"If we could but paint with the hand as we see with the eye!" Someone spoke behind me. Him again! What was it about his voice that turned my middle into a lump of hot melted cheese? "What color are you going to paint the rest of the shrubbery?" he asked.

"What?" When I glanced up and saw the white-spattered foliage, I overlooked momentarily the man standing beside me. A four-foot section of forsythia my mother had planted by the fence was covered with paint.

"Don't worry. I think we can trim it." Jericho Scott smiled as he removed a paint-specked limb. I watched him without a word.

". . . your hedge clippers?" he was saying. "A few whacks should do it."

"Oh. They're in the shed, I think." I gave myself mental demerits for blundering. This man had seen me at my absolute worst—and nude, besides. He must think I had the IQ of a turnip.

He touched my face with a fingertip. "There's paint on your cheek here . . . and a little smudge there in your hair."

His fingers were warm as he brushed the strand of hair from my forehead, and I felt as if my face had been dipped in hot tallow. My shirt had a rip in it, my arms were streaked with paint, and I suddenly didn't know what to do with my hands. I grabbed a can and sprayed some more.

While Jericho trimmed away the white-flecked leaves, I told him about the man in Chloe's apartment. "You missed the excitement last night," I said. "I practically came face-to-face with him before he slipped out the front way."

He turned to look at me. "Well, you know what they say: A mouse that hath but one hole is quickly taken."

I laughed. "Says who?"

"I forget." Jericho frowned. "Did they find out who it was?"

"Not yet." I sprayed the last of the paint and tossed the can aside. "Whoever it was wanted something from Chloe's office. Could've been the copy for her next column."

"What makes you think that?"

I knew then I had said too much. "Why are you here, Jericho Scott?"

He smiled and came to sit beside me on the grass. "I

can see you're much too shrewd for me. Okay, I might as well come clean. I'm working on a novel, a story of intrigue; it's set in a small town and that's why I'm here—to get the feel of it."

"But why Sweetsprings? Is it because of that girl who was killed here?"

He pulled up a fistful of grass and let it sift through his fingers, examined the dark earth at his feet as if he were counting the granules. "I heard about that, but no; this just seemed a quiet place where I could write in peace. I used to drive through now and then, and someone told me your neighbor needed some help." He smiled. "So we worked out a deal: She lets me stay in her carriage house and I look after her property—at least for the rest of the summer."

I didn't ask him what then, although I wanted to. I did ask him why Miss Baby Kennemore didn't hire her own nephew to take care of the grounds. "From what I've heard about Dillard Moore, he seems able-bodied enough."

"I think she tried that. It didn't work." He frowned. "Just what have you heard about Dillard Moore?"

"Not much, and nothing good," I said. "Was this some kind of family arrangement, or did Miss Baby ask him here?"

He shook his head. "I doubt it. In fact, I think she's a little afraid of him."

Next door Eulonia pulled into her driveway, slammed the car door, and clomped into the house to remind me, no doubt, that she had been to church and I hadn't. Jericho and I looked at one another and laughed but neither of us made any effort to move. In fact, we sat there talking for at least another hour until I got a cramp in my foot. I approved of his dark, good looks, his slow, thoughtful smile—and the fact that he was the exact opposite of Mac McCullough.

"How do you feel about Chinese food?" Jericho asked, standing to brush the grass from his pants. "I hear they've opened a new restaurant just outside of town."

I thought of Sudie's parting words: "Remember to keep your doors locked. We don't know a thing about that guy next door." And a nagging voice inside of me was bellowing BEWARE! Besides, I didn't even like Chinese food.

"I'd love it," I said.

Chapter Six

I spent the afternoon doing laundry, then showered and put on the new African print cotton I'd never had a chance to wear. I was beginning to tan a little and the sun had turned my blond hair even lighter. I didn't look so bad; at least it was an improvement on the torn, paint-spattered shirt.

Jericho and I were sipping drinks later on the porch when we heard the screen door slam at Eulonia's, and Shelba Jean, in a black French-cut bathing suit, flounced across the yard with a beach towel over her shoulder.

"You're not going out to that lake today?" her mother called after her. "After what happened here last night, and with poor Chloe lying up there in the morgue. And I'd think you'd at least have the decency to wear a proper suit."

"My going to the lake like this isn't going to worry Chloe." Shelba Jean slid under the wheel of her white Toyota. "You're the one it bothers, Mother, and I wish just this once you'd leave me alone." The noise from her revving engine sounded like an exclamation mark.

"And it wouldn't hurt you to go to the church supper with me—after all it is Sunday." Eulonia's words came out in a plaintive monotone, but her daughter didn't hear them. She was gone.

Jericho frowned after her. "Good lord, wouldn't you like to smack that kid with a giant-sized flyswatter?"

"I'd pay for the privilege," I said, "but I really don't envy her having to live with her mother. Eulonia had Shelba Jean kind of late, and sometimes she can be as high-pressured as a fire hose!"

He laughed. "The old man walk out on them?"

"No—believe it or not! He was killed in some kind of construction accident when Shelba Jean was a baby, and Eulonia's had to raise her alone. Shelba Jean's all she has. She'll wait up for her now until she comes dragging home again. Just wait and see."

"Oh, well, somebody once said the wildest colts make the best horses, but in this case I kind of doubt it." Jericho shook his head. "Poor Eulonia! I'm afraid she's in for a long wait."

But Eulonia's house was dark long before I finally went to bed that night. The restaurant had turned out okay after all and we stayed longer than I expected. Shagg Henry was there with some of his friends from the high school faculty, and they insisted we share their table.

"I hear you had some excitement next door again last night," one of the teachers said over dinner.

Shagg looked at me across the table. "What happened? Why didn't you call?"

I told him as I sipped my tea, "I think we scared him away."

"He was after something. . . . Wonder what it was," Shagg said.

"I think it was the copy for Chloe's next column," I said, looking about me. "It wasn't due until Monday, and it could've been in her desk."

"Not if she mailed it." Sharon Poteet reached for an egg roll and offered half to Shagg. The two of them had dated off and on for the three years she'd been teaching here, and I think she was hoping it would develop into something more.

"But what would Chloe have in her column that anybody would want to steal?" Shagg asked.

"Or kill for?" Sharon reminded him.

"Wait a minute." Jericho pushed his plate aside. "Did Chloe Applegate have anything to do with whatever's going on up there in the woods?"

Some of the teachers exchanged puzzled glances. "Heavens no, I wouldn't think so," one of them said.

"And what about the Lucas girl?"

"Etta," Sharon said. "I just don't know about Etta. If she was, I doubt if she took it seriously. Life was kind of a game to her."

Jericho crumbled a fortune cookie into pieces. "Not anymore," he said.

"Do you know of any connection between Chloe and Etta Lucas?" he asked me later as we put off saying good night.

"I can't think of any. It's a small town—they knew each other; that's all." I stretched and yawned. It was no use trying to hide it: I was sleepy—but I wasn't ready to go to sleep. The screen porch was dark and quiet, and I was glad it was just the two of us here together. For a while I had been afraid Shagg and his friends were going to drop by after dinner, and once thought I saw his car drive slowly past. But apparently he got my wordless message when we parted earlier.

I leaned back against the cushions of the old porch glider. They smelled musty no matter how long they aired in the sun. I had no idea what time it was, and didn't really care.

Jericho Scott seemed content just to be near me as we sat quietly together listening to a frog chorus in the grass, and once in a while when our hands touched, he laced his fingers in mine. It was a nice feeling. It was more than a nice feeling, but why didn't he take me in his arms? Was something wrong with me? With him?

"You'd better throw me out of here," he said at last. "It's late, and I promised Miss Baby I'd weed that forty-acre garden tomorrow."

"Right," I said, but I didn't move.

"Come on." He pulled me gently to my feet and walked

with me to the door. I drew away from him. Apparently he wasn't attracted to me, or . . . God forbid—maybe he was gay!

He wasn't gay. I knew his eyes were on me, felt them drawing me nearer. His arms went around me, his hands warm and firm against my back as I knew they would be. "Jane," he said. And that was all—for a while.

I smiled as I went up to bed. For at least twelve amazing hours I hadn't thought once of Mac McCullough, who had announced the week before our wedding that we had grown apart! Putting off sleep, I read for a while before I saw the lights go out in the carriage house across the Kennemore orchard. Was he thinking now of me? Probably not. Watch it, Jane! I told myself. Don't play on the railroad track! But I knew I wouldn't listen.

Since Sudie was still out, I left a light for her downstairs, happy that the usually stodgy Ralph had elected to stay longer. And later, when the sound of humming woke me, I thought my friend's fiancé might have celebrated with a few too many drinks.

I sat up in bed and listened. Someone—a man—was crooning that same familiar hymn, and it seemed to be coming from the yard next door.

Sudie's bed was still empty, and I glanced at the clock on the dresser. It was almost 2 A.M. Without turning on a light, I knelt by the window and felt the soft rush of night air against my face.

"Rock of Ages, cleft for me . . ." A fragment of melody drifted through the darkness. The sound of it made me feel vulnerable and sad. Who kept singing that depressing hymn in the small hours of the morning, and where on earth *was* Sudie? Then a screen door flapped shut, and for a brief flash of time, a light shone in the window across the way.

I yawned and rubbed my eyes. I was sleepy, but surely I wasn't dreaming! For a split second I saw a man wearing sunglasses and with dark bushy hair in Eulonia Moody's kitchen!

• • •

The slamming of a car door on the street below startled me back to reality. How long had I nodded, lost in a vague, predawn limbo, arms still folded on the window-sill, with a bothersome pain in my neck? Eulonia's kitchen window remained a dark square in the slate gray night, and the muted sound of a motor idling intruded on the silence.

The driver of the vehicle in the driveway had thoughtfully extinguished his headlights, switching them on after he backed into the street. I smiled. How like Ralph to conceal his alley cat hour of arrival! What would the neighbors say? Poor Ralph! He would have a long drive ahead of him if he meant to go back to Atlanta tonight, I thought as I watched the glowing taillights diminish. But why was Ralph Mitchell driving a pickup truck—and a rather battered one at that? It seemed unlikely transportation for one as conservative as Sudie's image-conscious fiancé.

Pretending sleep, I huddled under the covers, listening to my friend's soft tread on the stairs. I waited until Sudie had settled in bed and turned her pillow for the third time before I asked, "Ralph trade in his BMW?" But Sudie didn't answer. Somewhere close by a motorcycle growled to life and putt-putted away into what was left of the night.

Sudie was still asleep when I came home for lunch the next day after working all morning at the store. Stretched out on her back with one arm across her face, she slept in the shirt she had worn the night before. I smiled. How un-Sudie-like! And it was almost half past noon. I gave the covers a shake. "Give up, Sleeping Beauty, the prince took a hike."

She opened her eyes and turned over. "Go away!"

But my curiosity was relentless. "No way. Come on, there's fresh cantaloupe—I'll even stir us up an omelet." I left her to battle the morning blahs and rushed downstairs to start the coffee. Maybe the smell of it would give her an incentive.

But the eggs were cooling by the time Sudie dragged herself into the kitchen.

"Must have been some night. Did you and Ralph go coon hunting?" I almost spilled my coffee laughing at the idea.

Sudie tasted her omelet and frowned. "Did I miss something?"

"Look, Sudie, I saw it." I slowly buttered a muffin.

"Saw what?"

"The truck—the pickup truck! Let's see, it was somewhere between the man with bushy hair singing 'Rock of Ages' and the motorcycle sputtering under my window."

"I hope you're going to explain that," she said, barely covering a yawn.

I told her about Eulonia's nocturnal visitor. "And that's not the first time he's been there," I said. "I heard somebody humming that same song the night before Chloe was killed."

"Probably some freakish friend of Shelba Jean's," Sudie said. "Sounds like her kind of date."

"With Mama Eulonia right there in the same house? He wouldn't get past the back steps." I put down my fork. "Now it's your turn for answers. You weren't out with Ralph last night, were you?"

Sudie examined the salt shaker as if she'd never seen it before.

"It was that man from the garage, wasn't it? Come on, Sudie! It's me—Jane—remember? Something's wrong, isn't it? Why can't you tell me?"

"Why? You seem to know everything already." Sudie scraped congealed egg into the sink. "And you're biting your fingernails again!"

I sat at the table for a long time after she left. Sudie and I had been close friends since grammar school; we never kept secrets from one another. Now she was treating me like a stranger. Why should I care if she dumped boring old Ralph? Frankly, I'd never been excited about him in the first place; and apparently neither had she.

I glanced at the Kennemores' before I left the house,

but the red Mustang was not in its customary parking place nor had I heard from Jericho Scott. I walked a little faster than usual on my way back to town, glad to have the activity at the store to occupy my mind. I had only been there a few minutes when Eulonia plodded in the back door with a little container of strawberries.

"You said something about wanting some the other day," she said placing them on the counter with a put-upon sigh. "And I had to go by the produce stand anyway; Shelba Jean does love their peaches."

I was curious to know when Shelba Jean got in from the lake and if she had any connection with the hymn-humming man. I counted out the money for the berries, wondering how to mention it tactfully, and decided there wasn't a way. "I could have sworn I saw a man in your kitchen late last night!" I blurted, throwing caution aside. "Looked like he had long, thickish hair, and he was humming 'Rock of Ages.' " After all, I told myself, with a murder victim right next door, Eulonia should know the truth.

But Eulonia Moody didn't much care for the truth. I could tell by the way she drew in her breath and expelled it slowly, fixing me with a don't-bother-me look. "I expect it was me," she said finally. "I was on the cleanup committee for the church supper last night, and you know how it is—most of them walked out without a fare-thee-well leaving me to do all the dirty work!" Eulonia leaned heavily on the counter. "I like to never got through, and my feet hurt so I couldn't sleep when I did get home. I just turned on the radio and mixed myself up a batch of that instant pudding." Her hand moved from her hair to the collar of her blouse. "I reckon Shelba Jean slept right through all my puttering about."

I was glad somebody did, but I didn't say so. "And a little while later," I added, "it sounded like somebody took off on a motorcycle—right under my window."

Eulonia shook her head as she started out the way she had come. "One of those ragtags out on the highway," she muttered. But I thought she looked worried. The woman's purple polyester skirt was nappy with wear and her shoes were run down at the heels. Eulonia had money— she had to. Everybody in town joked about how Eulonia Moody never spent a dime, yet she had bought that snippy little Shelba Jean an expensive new car for graduation. It didn't make sense.

"Have you heard anything about Chloe's killer?" I called after her. "I don't suppose they've caught him yet?"

"No, and not likely to, either. Same one who murdered that little Lucas girl—you can bet on it."

Something in her voice stirred my compassion. Eulonia Moody was, above all, a mother, and no matter how annoying Shelba Jean appeared to be, she was probably her mother's main reason for living. If anything happened to Shelba Jean, Eulonia would be devastated. And Chloe Applegate had lived under the same roof.

I glanced at my watch after Eulonia left. It was almost three o'clock—plenty of time for Fred O'Leary to have picked up his mail. I scribbled "Be right back" on a piece of cardboard and stuck it in the window before locking the door behind me. The air felt heavy and humid, and heat rose from the pavement as I hurried down the street.

Fred O'Leary typed something into his word processor while talking to somebody over the phone. He frowned when he saw me and made a motion for me to wait. I leaned on the waist-high counter, looking for anything that might be Chloe Applegate's last column, and listened to his muttered end of the conversation.

"Well, they know what killed Chloe," he said, hanging up the receiver. "Now, if I can just find her column, we might have a paper this week."

"She drowned, didn't she?" I never wanted to swim in my neighbor's pool again!

Fred gulped what was left of his Diet Coke and shook his head. "Hit on the head with a croquet mallet. She was dead before she hit the water." He shuffled papers on his desk and poked about in a drawer. "Now where'd I put that damned thing?"

"How do they know it was a croquet mallet?"

"They found it. It was in that little covered area next to the pool. The Kennemores kept lawn games in there, badminton sets—stuff like that. The mallet still had Chloe's blood on it, but they couldn't get any prints."

I felt sick. I had heard the police out by the pool the day after Chloe was found, but I couldn't bring myself to ask what they were doing or to enter the area where Chloe might have died.

Now Fred was on his hands and knees searching beneath his littered desk. "You don't see a long white envelope, do you?" he asked, dusting off his hands. "I'd just come back from the post office when the phone rang and some dang fool told me my trash can out back was on fire." He scowled at me. "Somebody's idea of a joke, I reckon. There wasn't any fire out there!"

"Did it sound like a man or a woman?"

"More like a man; could've been a woman though, I guess."

"Did you have a chance to read it before the call?" I held my breath.

The editor mopped his red face. "Didn't even have time to open it." He ruffled through a stack of junk mail on the counter. "Now where do you reckon that damn thing got to? I could've sworn I put it on my desk . . . must've dropped it on the way from the post office!"

But I knew Chloe's column hadn't been lost. And I thought I knew who had taken it.

Chapter Seven

I stood alone in the doorway, watching the rain pelt the streets as a brief summer shower darkened the skies that afternoon. In spite of the electric lighting, the empty shop looked unusually dim, and each tiny noise from the storeroom behind me seemed threatening. I rubbed my arms for warmth and sifted through the dress rack for ideas on a new window display. Only a few customers had drifted in that afternoon, and the silence of the old building was almost oppressive. For all I knew, Chloe's murderer might be someone familiar—someone right here on Main Street. The sudden jangling of the doorbell caught me off guard and I jumped instinctively, then felt like a complete idiot when I saw it was only Shagg.

"Frightening, isn't it?" He made a face. "Scares me every time I look in the mirror."

I tossed a dress over my arm and turned my back to look through the costume jewelry. My hand trembled as I picked out bracelets and a necklace, and I knew he could read the relief in my face. "Sorry," I said, avoiding his eyes. "Must be the storm."

"Or the fact that your neighbor was murdered with a croquet mallet, no less—I heard! Come on, it's after five o'clock. Lock up this place and I'll treat you to dinner and a movie."

The rain had let up and I was only too glad to leave the depressing store behind me and walk along beside Shagg down the now-steaming sidewalks. Yet somehow I felt his offer was not as impromptu as it seemed.

Shagg paused to look in the window of the furniture store on the corner. "You two must have had a good time last night . . . saw that guy's car in your driveway when I passed there on my way home."

So it had been Shagg's car I'd seen. I smiled. "Since when do you pass my house on the way to yours?"

He seemed to be studying intently a set of redwood lawn furniture that had been in the window the summer before. "Just checking, that's all." He shrugged. "He seems nice enough, but what do you really know about him? After all, Chloe was found right there in that pool!"

I caught his hand and pulled him along. "Give me a break, Shagg. You sound just like my mother."

His face turned as red as his hair. "Well, somebody has to look after you!"

"Then you'll have to get in line," I said. "Sudie has already—"

"Speaking of—" Shagg stopped so short I almost ran into him. "Isn't that Sudie over there in the park? Who's that with her?"

A small park ringed with oaks separated the business district from the residential area of town, and Sudie Gaines stood on the stone bridge spanning the pond with the bearded man from the garage. I felt something akin to déjà vu. This was where I had seen the man before—on this same bridge—with Chloe Applegate! I watched Sudie lean over the water and throw bread crumbs to the ducks, while Nelson Fain sat on the parapet, apparently deep in serious conversation.

"That's what I've been meaning to tell you," I began, but before I could stop him, Shagg was tugging me forward, down the winding pathway to the bridge, calling to Sudie as he ran.

Surprise! Surprise! Sudie didn't seem at all glad to see us, and looked as if she wished she were anywhere else. I regretted putting her on the spot. . . . Oh, well, actually I kind of enjoyed it. After all, what else could I do? It was her own fault for acting like such an ass.

"Well, looks like this is my afternoon to run into everybody I know," Sudie said, watching soggy bread disappear beneath the surface of the water.

I wanted to push her under with it. Instead, I found myself smiling stiffly, as if I were meeting a stranger. The two men shook hands as they were introduced. Shagg wore his usual friendly smile, but Nelson Fain looked decidedly uncomfortable, I thought. And they stood there making small talk. Imagine, small talk—with Sudie. I refused to become involved.

Nelson became more animated when he pointed out a scattering of dead trees in a small wooded area at one end of the park where he said woodpeckers nested and fed. He seemed to know what he was talking about, and Shagg pretended interest, although I knew he didn't care a whit.

But Sudie did. Now I realized what the two of them had in common. I watched her face as the group moved off the bridge and walked slowly up the pathway. She was hanging on every word. Sudie had been interested in birds since high school, and I had even known her to crawl out of bed in the predawn hours to observe them while normal people slept. This time, however, Sudie was interested in more than birds.

When we came to an intersection in the paths she made a hasty exit for town, muttering something about an appointment with the dentist. I asked her if she wanted to meet Shagg and me for dinner later on, but she said she had to give a couple of piano lessons and didn't know when she'd be through. "I'll see you tonight," she called back to me, walking a little faster. I'd never seen Sudie Gaines in such a rush to get to the dentist. I lifted my hand to wave, but she had already started across the street.

Nelson left us at the top of the park steps and hurried in the opposite direction. Shagg stared after him, frowning. "What in the hell was that all about?"

I told him as we walked. "Something's wrong. Sudie has never acted like this. Obviously she's running around on Ralph—but why all the secrecy?"

Shagg shook his head. "They're hiding something, couldn't you tell? Couldn't wait to get away from us."

"I know I've seen that man before," I said. "He was standing on that same bridge with Chloe Applegate. I probably wouldn't have noticed it, but she had on some kind of wild purple and green outfit and he looked kind of drab beside her."

"When?"

"A couple of weeks ago. I came home for a few days to bring some of my things, and I was on my way to the shop to see Alice."

"I don't think he wanted anyone to know he was meeting Sudie," Shagg said. "Look, there's his truck parked on a side street."

I watched the bearded mechanic get behind the wheel of his pickup. "Wish we could follow him."

"We can. I left my car at the recreation center—it's only a couple of blocks from here. If I run, I can be back before he gets too far. Stay here and see where he goes."

I heard him disappear down the driveway behind me and knew he was taking a shortcut through somebody's yard. The dusty blue truck moved down the street and stopped at the light on the corner. I watched it dutifully, almost afraid to blink.

"Well, Jane! I thought that was you. And how are you faring with your folks way over there in Europe?" Mrs. Huffstetler, who lived in the house on the corner, wheeled her garbage to the curb. "I do hope they're going to Scotland. Why, when Arthur and I were there in seventy-eight . . . or was it seventy-nine . . ."

I made appropriate noises, afraid to look away. I saw the truck go down another block and turn right at the next corner.

". . . and prices are so high," Mrs. Huffstetler went on. ". . . stayed in a lot of those bed and breakfast places, but my word, we nearly froze to death!"

Brakes squealed as Shagg rounded the corner and I managed to jump inside the car as he slowed in front of me, leaving Mrs. Huffstetler standing openmouthed on the curbside. "Well, they'll hear about this at the garden club tomorrow!" I said, fighting to pull the door shut.

"We're going to feel pretty silly if Nelson Fain is only going to the grocery store," I said as we caught sight of the truck up ahead of us.

Shagg slowed the car, then frowned as we watched the truck make another turn. "I don't think we'll have to worry about that," he said, "unless they've built a super-market in the Widow's Woods."

Somber trees still dripped from the recent rain as Shagg and I left the car by the side of the road and picked our way into the dense thicket. Nelson Fain had driven his truck into what looked like an old logging road and disappeared from view. I stood in the tall grass and listened to the sound of his engine grow fainter until everything was quiet except for the plop-plopping of water from the leaves overhead.

"Come on or we'll lose him." Shagg took my hand and I allowed him to lead me along, looking neither to the left nor the right. The woods were cold and dark—even in summer, and they gave me the same feeling I got when I looked at a snake. I told Shagg that.

"You were the one who wanted to follow this guy— remember? Maybe he's just bird-watching." He pushed aside an overhanging branch and released a shower of raindrops. "Besides, I think you've been listening to too many widow tales. That old woman's been dead for years, and most of those stories are exaggerated anyway."

I didn't answer. I felt as if I were suffocating. The damp smell of earth and decay rose to meet me, surrounded me like an invisible shroud. The place seemed steeped in something akin to melancholy, but worse—much worse.

65

Still holding fast to my hand, Shagg plunged through a small clearing; his eyes were intense, his face had the look of a hunter. I pulled my hand away.

Suddenly he gripped my arm. "Look, there's his truck! He must be close by." Shagg held me against him. "Listen."

Somewhere not too far away someone waded through damp leaves on the forest floor, obviously unaware that he was being followed. "Wait here; I'll see where he goes." Shagg moved behind a tree and was gone. I was glad when he drew away from me. His body was hot and damp, and my arm tingled from his grasp. What was wrong with me? Suddenly the warm, witty friend I knew and loved had seemed like a stranger. I backed against a giant sycamore, felt its scaly bark beneath my fingers. I had been *afraid* of Shagg Henry.

I wanted to run, to tear through the vines and brambles until I reached the light. But the forbidding trees guarded me, penned me in, and cloaked me in their shadow. I had an irrational feeling that this place would remain forever dark, even after the trees were gone. And from somewhere not too far away, I sensed I was being watched by a pair of malicious yellow eyes.

Shagg seemed to appear from nowhere. "Hurry, he's coming! We have to get out of here!" His abrupt whisper made me jump, but I was glad to scramble after him across the brown mottled ground.

Again in the sunlight I felt almost ashamed of myself for my peculiar reaction to the Widow's Woods. Shagg was once more the familiar friend from childhood—loyal and good-natured, if a bit unpredictable, and I felt as if I owed him an apology. But he must not have noticed my odd behavior because he waved my explanations aside, intent on herding me back to the car.

"I don't think he saw us," he said, pulling back onto the road with a spattering of mud. "If we can just make it to the crossroads on the other side of this hill, he'll never know we were here."

I leaned back against the seat and let the sun beat down

yellow and warm on my face. "Where was he? What was he doing in there?"

"Over there close to that devil's ring or whatever it is where those kids were messing around. He seemed to be looking for something." Shagg turned left onto a gravel road and dipped out of sight just as the truck whizzed past at the intersection.

"Well?" I asked. "Do you think he found it?"

Shagg frowned. "No, I don't think so," he said. "But he definitely wasn't bird-watching!"

I had seen newspaper photographs of the circle of stones, supposedly used in the satanic rituals. Police had found thick mold beneath each of the five large stones that formed a pentagram within the circle; and in the center of the ring stood what was believed to be a large altar rock and remains of a fire pit. Shelba Jean and her friends claimed to have discovered the ritual site and gone there as a graduation night lark, but if they hadn't laid out the stones, then who had?

I knew the pentagram was a symbol of Satan and that part of the satanic ritual was the letting of blood—which would explain the excessive mold beneath the rocks. I wondered if it had something to do with the beheading of the two pets. Instinctively I moved closer to Shagg as the sun dropped behind a cloud. I was glad when we drove back into town.

Chapter Eight

Papa Sam got home from his fishing trip at noon the next day. At about ten after, my phone rang at the shop.

"Why the devil didn't you get in touch with me?" he said. "Is it true about Chloe Applegate? I hear you were the one who found her."

"It's true," I said. From the tone of his voice you would have thought I'd whacked Chloe over the head myself, and that I did it just to provoke him.

"Get over here," he said, and hung up.

I found him in the living room, watching a baseball game on television and eating boiled peanuts. The sword that always hung over the mantel was conspicuously absent. He looked up from the tackle box in his lap, a bright orange lure in his hand. His friend Cooter Edwards dozed on the sofa with a copy of *Field and Stream* over his face. "I don't suppose they've caught the lowlife who did it?" my grandfather said.

I kissed the top of his balding head. "Not yet." I sniffed. "You've been smoking those vile cigars again."

"Don't change the subject. I don't like you over there in that house by yourself. There's plenty of room right here."

"I know, Papa Sam." I touched his arm. "But I'm fine—really. Sudie's staying with me."

"Oh, Sudie! Well, I feel a whole lot better." He concentrated on tying a feather onto something that looked green and slimy. A fat black cat leapt onto his lap and batted the lure with a paw. Samuel Lightbourne shoved it away with a gentle hand. "How much does Sudie weigh now? Ninety-five? A hundred? And five-feet-three at the most! What kind of protection is that?"

I didn't let on that I was concerned about Sudie myself —but it wasn't over her weight and size. Shagg and I had decided the night before that Sudie should be told about Nelson's mysterious trip to the Widow's Woods, but she had been asleep when I got home and was gone by the time I was fully awake this morning.

"We have neighbors," I reminded him.

"Uh-huh. Same neighbors Chloe had." Papa Sam closed the lid on his tackle box and set it aside. "How long's it been since that little Lucas girl was murdered? Must be three—four months now, and police don't know a damn thing more than they did." He shook his head. "Now it's Chloe. Good lookin' woman—smart, too. Don't reckon they've buried her yet. Who's in charge of the funeral?"

Cooter mumbled something from underneath his magazine. I had almost forgotten he was there.

"Who? What'd you say?" Papa Sam's feet hit the floor.

"I said, Eulonia, I reckon," Cooter answered, letting the magazine slide to the floor. "Nobody else left."

"Well, that's a hell of a fix! So damn stingy she'll have her buried in a pine box, and she's not even kin at that."

My grandfather had tangled with Eulonia Moody when she had first come to Sweetsprings fifteen years ago and taken a job at McClain's Drugstore. That was back when they still delivered, and Eulonia had sent him the wrong brand of cigars three times in a row. They finally moved her to the cosmetics department. Papa Sam said when folks got a good look at Eulonia, they'd be willing to pay for whatever makeup it took to keep it from happening to them.

Eulonia Moody was a strange one all right. I had a feeling she knew all along about the man I had seen in her kitchen, and that she was covering for somebody. But I didn't know who or why; when it came right down to it, I really didn't know much at all about the woman next door.

"Where did the Moodys live before they came here?" I asked.

"Lord, I don't know! Came here when that little gal was not much more than a baby. Husband was killed in some kind of accident—somewhere down near the coast. Wish to hell she'd stayed there!" Papa Sam trimmed a cigar into the ashtray and fumbled for matches.

"Better watch that cussing, Papa Sam," I said. "They'll throw you out of the Baptist Church."

"Can't throw out somebody who don't never go." A short round woman in a blue cotton dress snatched the ashtray from my grandfather and whisked it into the kitchen.

"Ruby worries about my health," my grandfather said loudly. "I think she covets my body. . . . Next thing you know, she'll be after my liquor."

Ruby Lovejoy paused in the kitchen doorway, her face as red as her name. "You hush up, now, Sam Lightbourne!" But her prim mouth twitched in a smile. She had come to work for Papa Sam after my grandmother died, and during her first few months of keeping house, had walked out on him an average of twice a week. I didn't blame her.

"She's right, Papa Sam," I said. "You don't take care of yourself." I sat on the arm of his chair. "Look at those peanuts you're eating. All that salt can't be good for you."

Mrs. Lovejoy bustled through with a broom. "That's what I keep telling him. Nasty, soggy things!"

Papa Sam tossed another nut into his mouth. "I won't pester you about staying alone," he said to me, "if you'll let me enjoy my vices in peace."

"I'll think about it." I stood and went to the mantel. "Where's the sword, Papa Sam?"

He seemed suddenly immersed in the ball game. Cooter made great work out of shelling a peanut.

"Papa Sam?"

"Hmm? Oh . . . just haven't gotten around to cleaning it."

I started to say something, but his eyes kept me from it. I got the distinct idea that the housekeeper's being there had something to do with my grandfather's deception. I waited until Ruby Lovejoy had gone outside to sweep the porch before I mentioned it again. "Now, tell me about the sword," I said. "It isn't here, is it?"

He shook his head. "I haven't seen it since I took it down to polish over a month ago. Then your mama came by and dragged me home to dinner, and the next day Cooter and I left for a fishing trip." He sighed. "When I got back the next week, it was gone."

"But why didn't you say something? Do the police know it's missing?"

Cooter lifted an eyebrow. "He thinks Ruby took it."

Papa Sam glared at his old friend. "Not Ruby, Coot. You know better'n that!"

"Then who?" I asked.

My grandfather lowered his voice—or tried to. "She has a grandson—Nathan—you've seen him: about sixteen and all nose and ears. I've always thought he was a right good kid, but lately he's taken to running with a pretty rough lot. I know Ruby worries about him."

"But why would he take the sword?"

Papa Sam glanced out the window where the plump housekeeper wielded the broom as if she meant to sweep away the porch, floor and all. "The few times he's been here the boy always admired it, wanted to hold it and all. Still, I don't think he'd take it on his own, unless one of the others put him up to it."

"Do you think Mrs. Lovejoy knows?" I asked.

"Good lord, no! She'd drag him in here feet first, quoting scripture all the way."

• • •

72

I smiled as I told Shagg about it when he came by the store later that day. "I can't imagine why the boy wanted it," I said. "I just hope Papa Sam can find a way to get it back."

"If anybody can, it will be your grandpa." Shagg offered me a Lifesaver. "Have you talked with Sudie yet?"

I shook my head. "I think she took her grandmother to the doctor today. She left while I was still in the shower. Shagg, do you really think Nelson Fain could be involved in all this mess?"

He shrugged. "Beats me, but I think Sudie knows more about him than she wants to admit. Wonder where she met him? They seem an unlikely pair."

"She wants me to believe she met him last week when he relined her brakes, but I think she's known him a whole lot longer." I rang up three pairs of stockings for a customer and waited until the door closed behind her. "And there's something else," I said. "I think it was Nelson Fain in Chloe's apartment the other night."

"Are you sure? I thought you said you didn't see him."

"It happened so fast I couldn't be positive, but he was about that size, and he had a beard."

"My God, Jane!" Shagg looked like I'd just hauled off and slapped him. "Still, I don't believe our Saint Sudie would have anything to do with him if she even suspected he was involved with Chloe's murder." He picked up a bright red sandal from the display table and turned it over in his hands. "I wonder if sweet little Shelba Jean knows what's going on. She's been dating that creepy nephew of Miss Baby's—the one who's been staying there."

"Dillard Moore? Since when? Does Eulonia know?"

"She took him to the prom, and I've seen them together a couple of times since. I don't think Eulonia has a whole lot of control over what that kid does anymore. And how do we know she isn't mixed up in this herself?"

"Oh, come on, Shagg! I don't like the woman, but I've known her since I was a child. I really don't think she had

73

anything to do with Chloe's murder—or with that prowler, either. The poor thing was scared to death."

He laughed. "If that man had gotten a good look at Eulonia, it would've been the other way around." Shagg glanced at his watch. "Look, I've gotta run; I'm supposed to coach a softball team in about five minutes. Just promise me you'll talk with Sudie, okay? And if I see her, I'll do the same."

Later, I had sort of a tranquil feeling just thinking about our conversation. Maybe Shagg Henry was growing up at last. I didn't even hear the bell jangle when Miss Baby Kennemore came in to buy her summer supply of cotton camisoles.

"How are you, dear? I know this must be a trying time for you with all these dreadful things going on." The frail woman placed her heavy navy handbag on the counter and her narrow pink hand on mine. "Are you and Sudie all right over there? I've tried to call several times, but of course I forgot you'd be here at the store."

I laid a box of the dainty chambray garments on the counter. "We're doing all right, thank you; and we've thought of you, too. It hasn't been an easy time for any of us, has it?" I wanted to ask if her nephew had returned, but I couldn't think of a way to bring it up after what Jericho had said.

"Have you heard from your parents? How I envy them! I'd love to take another trip. See the pyramids again, the Colosseum—all those wonderful places I visited once before."

"Not yet," I said. "They'll probably call next week."

"They're going to be awfully upset when they hear about Chloe." Miss Baby looked as if she might begin to cry, and I didn't know if it was because of Chloe's death or the fact that she wasn't spending the summer in exotic lands.

"That's why I'm not going to tell them. What good would it do? It would only spoil their trip, and it's not going to bring back Chloe."

"I hope they'll hurry and find who did it," she said.

I nodded. "I can't imagine what Chloe was doing at your pool unless somebody lured her there. You know how she hated the water." I remembered Chloe's last column and the suggestion of Miss Baby's rumored romance. "I do miss Chloe," I said. "I realize she upset people sometimes with the silly things she wrote, but I don't think she meant any harm."

To my surprise Miss Baby laughed. "What a tease she was! I suppose you saw that column about my class reunion?"

I could only nod.

"That was her little prank, you see," Miss Baby went on. "All that hooey about rekindled love! I made the mistake of telling Chloe about a fellow in my class—Darwin Hinshaw—close to seven feet tall, red face, and pimples! The silly thing had a crush on me—just about drove me crazy—and I was so afraid he'd be there!"

I laughed. "And was he?"

"My goodness, no! I heard he married some girl from West Virginia and had about six or seven children. Probably couldn't afford to come if he put that bunch through college."

I rang up the purchases and put them into a bag. "Miss Baby, you still substitute some at the high school, don't you? What's going on with those kids over there? Are they really into satanism or just playing around with it?"

Almost unconsciously, she smoothed her hair. "I wish I knew. I don't fill in much anymore, but from what I hear, I suspect a few of them are experimenting with things better left alone." She braced her hands on the counter. "Why, just the other night a bunch of these hooligans spray-painted the numbers six-six-six on the side of that little brick church out on Wilsons' Ferry Road and tore down their sign out front."

"Six-six-six? What does that mean? Sounds like just plain vandalism to me."

"Why that's the devil's number—or so they say." Miss Baby accepted her purchases. "And you just try to check out a book on the supernatural at any of the libraries in this area . . . you won't find a one."

I frowned. "Why? What do you mean?"

"I mean most have been stolen—or checked out and not returned, and the few that remain have had most of their pages cut out!"

Chapter Nine

"Why would anybody want to do such a thing?" I asked Jericho that evening as we picnicked on the back porch.

He speared the last pickle in the jar. "Maybe somebody doesn't approve."

"Maybe," I said, "but I don't think so, and neither does Miss Baby."

Jericho finished off a drumstick and added the bone to the collection on his plate. "Does she know who's involved?"

"No, but I'll bet she could guess." I leaned back in the lounge chair and watched the sunset streak the sky in fluorescent pink and gold. At the edge of the yard the sprinkler swished with intermittent showers my mother's bold red zinnias, and on the near horizon the dark trees waited, watching. I glanced at Jericho, lazing across from me in the hammock, then looked quickly away. How could the world be so beautiful and so cruel?

Sudie had called earlier to say she had ignored her piano and her apartment long enough, and I was welcome to stay awhile with her. But as much as I disliked the idea of being in the house at Kennemore's Crossing alone, I decided to give it a try. Whatever brought about Chloe's death had nothing to do with me, I told myself. More than that, I think I wanted to prove to the town of Sweetsprings that Jane Cannon was a mature, rational adult—and quite capable, thank you, of looking after herself. It also gave me a chance to be alone with Jericho Scott.

It was dark inside the kitchen as we cleared away the remains of our supper, but I sensed the warmth and strength of him beside me. As I reached for the light switch inside the door, he put out his hand and touched my bare arm. It was as simple as that. If this is Prince Charming, I thought as we kissed, please don't let him turn into a frog right now!

Then from somewhere past the borders of fantasyland, I heard a dreadful noise. Someone pounded on the front door, almost in rhythm with the pounding in my temples, and Eulonia Moody burst into the hallway—about as welcome as a cockroach at Sunday dinner.

"I thought you'd never hear me!" she twanged, squinting past me at Jericho. "Something awful's happened! They've arrested Miss Baby's nephew! The police think he's the one you saw in Chloe's apartment the other night, and they're holding him down at the jail."

"Shagg says he's seen that man with Shelba Jean," I told Jericho as we left the police station later that night. "But I'm not sure he's the one I saw the other night. This guy Dillard's been hanging around with some of the younger crowd; in fact, I heard he was one of that group that set fire to the woods on graduation night."

"I've seen him over at the Moodys' a couple of times," Jericho said. "But he's older than the Moody girl, isn't he? Must be in his twenties at least."

"Poor Miss Baby! She's going to feel awful about this! I wonder why she wasn't there."

"Maybe they haven't told her yet. Anyway, it won't hurt him to cool his heels in jail awhile. He'll be out soon enough."

I yawned. It was late and my eyes burned from lack of sleep. I hadn't been able to positively identify Dillard Moore as the intruder. The dark stubble on his chin could scarcely be called a beard, but he was about the same size as the man I'd seen, and the police had found a key to Chloe's apartment in the pocket of his jeans when they picked him up for driving while intoxicated.

"Sure looks like he's our man to me," Jericho said as we stood in the parking lot beside town hall. "How does he explain having that key?"

"Says he found it. . . . Well, maybe he did."

Jericho tilted his head and looked at me. "Well, of course he *said* that, Jane."

I shrugged. "I'm not saying he doesn't look suspicious, but I just don't think he's the one. Besides, why would he need a key when Shelba Jean could have left the door open?"

Jericho nodded. "But you said Chloe kept a key under the flowerpot. Maybe he had a copy made."

"But what would Chloe Applegate have that he couldn't get at home? She didn't have any money, and I don't think her jewelry was expensive." As much as I wanted my world to be normal again, I preferred to be sure the right person was locked away.

Across the street the tall granite columns of the old post office loomed pale against the night. Next door the brownish brick of the small Episcopal church seemed even darker behind the camellias and protective wrought-iron fence. I had listened to stories under the big oak tree at the library on the corner; roller-skated on these walks, visited in the houses. I knew this town and its people. They were as much a part of my life as Papa Sam's stories and picnics at Bonners' Spring. And now the police had arrested my neighbor's nephew with Chloe's door key in his pocket. Maybe he held the key to her murder as well.

Why did I still feel afraid?

I locked my car doors as I drove the short distance home. The streets were deserted, and most of the houses dark. A few blocks from Kennemore's Crossing I heard the low rumble of a motorcycle, and a large, helmeted man roared past. I tried to signal to Jericho in the car behind me, but it was too dark. I stared at the man's profile as I drew up next to him at the light. I was sure it was the same man I had seen in Eulonia's kitchen.

When the light changed, the cyclist veered left into a side street, and I was tempted to follow. But what would I do if I caught him?

I had breakfast with Papa Sam the next morning before attending Chloe's funeral together. We ate our biscuits and muscadine preserves hurriedly, along with my grandpa's caldron-hot coffee. The funeral was scheduled for mid-morning, and we knew the church would be crowded.

It was. We sat near the front with Fred O'Leary and two others from *The Sweetsprings Sun*. I was surprised to see Eulonia and a sullen Shelba Jean file in last with a few of Chloe's out-of-town relatives. Sudie, I noticed, sat with Shagg on the other side of the crowded sanctuary. I found it hard to concentrate on the service for wondering about the man being held in the city jail. Did Dillard Moore have anything to do with Chloe's death? Because of his involvement with the younger crowd, I could more easily believe he was mixed up in the murder of Etta Lucas. But what could possibly be the connection between the respectable Chloe Applegate and this insignificant hoodlum, who, from all reports, did nothing but bring his family grief?

I heard several people sniffing back tears when the congregation stood to sing "Amazing Grace." It was hard to believe it was really Chloe beneath the blanket of white carnations—not the same Chloe who lavished affection on the children she taught or the Chloe who was always quick to share her cut flowers, her cookies, or a cool drink on a hot day. I felt a cold emptiness inside. Was the person responsible for my neighbor's death standing nearby weeping crocodile tears? As the pallbearers pushed the coffin up the aisle, I closed my eyes, glad the service was over at last.

Sudie waited at the foot of the stone steps. "Were you

okay last night, Jane? I heard they arrested that Dillard Moore." Her large brown eyes seemed watchful, I thought, as if she were searching for assurance.

"Fine," I said, taking her arm. "Listen, I want to talk to you."

"I know. Shagg told me. It's all right—really. Everything's okay."

"But who is he, Sudie? Who is Nelson Fain? And what's his connection with Chloe?"

Sudie's eyes narrowed. "With Chloe? What do you mean?"

"I saw them together not long before she was killed, and he might have been the man in her apartment the other night." I followed her to the edge of the lawn. "I guess Shagg told you he was looking for something in the Widow's Woods. . . . Sudie, I don't trust him!"

"It's not what you think; I can't talk about it now," Sudie said, turning away. "You're just going to have to believe me."

I stood looking after her. "It's not you I don't believe," I said.

Papa Sam, I saw, had already shed his coat and tie and was headed for his customary meeting place with cronies under the mimosa tree behind the town hall. His friend Cooter Edwards, however, had been commandeered by his wife Leola who caught up with me in the parking lot. "Surely you're not staying in that house out there alone?" she asked, lifting damp hair from her neck. "Your grandpa worries about you, Jane. You shouldn't be by yourself."

Was there a double meaning there? I tried not to sound offended. "I don't know why not," I said, "now that they've arrested that Moore boy. Besides, Papa Sam knows I'll call if I need him." But I won't, I thought. I was tired of feeling threatened in my own home and annoyed at having to depend on somebody else for protection.

"Jane, if you're going straight home, I wouldn't mind a ride." Eulonia stood beside me, dabbing her eyes with a yellowed linen handkerchief. Shelba Jean, I noticed, had escaped in the other direction in her sporty new car, leaving her mother to fend for herself.

"I know I ought to go on to the cemetery," Eulonia said, sinking back against the seat, "but, lordy, it's so hot, I'm already feeling dizzy—and my stomach's tied in a thousand knots!"

I pretended not to hear. "It was a nice service," I said, "and I'm glad it's over. Seems like it's been a year since Chloe—since all this happened."

"With the coroner's inquest and all, they couldn't get to it any sooner, and then we had to wait for those relatives to get here." Eulonia sighed. "I guess it's just as well she didn't have any close family left. I wouldn't want them to have to go through what I did with my Aaron—and poor little Shelba Jean no more than a baby." She sniffed a few times and blew her nose.

Oh, give me a break! I thought. I can't handle this. I glanced at Eulonia's puffy face. "It must have been hard for you. Where were you living when he—when that happened?"

Eulonia blinked at me over a wad of damp tissues. "Why Mullins, of course, where we always lived—before we came here, that is."

"Mullins, South Carolina?"

She nodded. "Little place down near the coast. You've probably never heard of it. I've nobody left there now—unless you count Cousin Myra."

"Do you still keep in touch?" I didn't really care if Eulonia's Cousin Myra had been shot into space, but as long as I kept her talking, maybe she wouldn't cry.

But Eulonia only grunted. "Haven't heard from her in years; reckon she still lives in that same old house on Aiken Street. Myra Updyke. They couldn't run the Methodist church there without her, or she thought they couldn't." And Eulonia came as close as I had ever seen her to laughing.

Still, I noticed, Eulonia twisted the strap of her pocketbook over and over in her hands. Between Chloe's death and having Shelba Jean to contend with, I guess she had a right to be upset. I hated to bring up the subject of the bushy-haired man, but I was tired of playing guessing games. "I saw that man again last night," I said as we turned into Kennemore's Crossing. "And this time I know it wasn't my imagination, Eulonia. It was the same man I saw in your kitchen, only this time he was on a motorcy-cle . . . and he was as close to me as you are now."

Eulonia made a sucking noise with her teeth. "Well, I reckon the whole town's gonna think I have a big ole' kinky-headed man sharing my kitchen—and who knows what else."

I tried not to smile. "I'm sorry, Eulonia, but I did see him, and he was the same man I saw in your window."

Eulonia fanned herself with her hand. "Don't you think I'd know it if some crazy person like that was prowling around my own kitchen?" She inched her other hand around the door handle for a quick escape. "I know you're nervous, being over there by yourself so much," she added sweetly. "Especially after—well—all your other problems. Why Shelba Jean and myself have been on pins and needles after what happened to poor Chloe, but it just isn't natural to go around seeing things that aren't there." She was out of the car almost before it came to a complete stop, slamming the door behind her. I had to laugh. I had never seen Eulonia move so fast.

"I can't make the woman believe me," I told Jericho later. "But after what happened to Chloe and with all this other stuff going on, she'd better accept the facts." I was making a halfhearted effort to weed my mother's flower border before it got too dark to see, and had a peculiar feeling I'd pulled up as many snapdragons as weeds.

"Maybe Eulonia knows more than you give her credit for," he said, looking at the house next door. "Whoever said children and fools can't lie didn't know Eulonia."

I pulled off my gardening gloves. "When do I get to read your manuscript?" It was the second time I'd asked.

He kissed me lightly. "Maybe later, when it's a little further along."

Or when it snows in July! I thought, watching him walk

across the lawn. The nearness of him gave me the sensation of being on a carnival ride. I even liked watching him walk. What was the matter with me? I slammed the door of the tool shed as the old hurt gnawed at me. Oh God, don't let it happen again! He was spending the evening writing, and I was glad. Things were moving much too fast.

Apparently Shagg thought so, too. "I wish you'd back off a little on this Jericho guy," he said when he dropped by later. "He hadn't been here but a few weeks before Chloe was killed, and he's staying right there where it happened."

"And so is Miss Baby," I reminded him. "Aren't you going to warn me about her?"

He shook his head at me. "And what are you doing here alone? Where's Sudie?"

"Have a heart, Shagg! I could use some time to myself. Besides, I'm a big girl now."

"I've noticed," he said. "And so has Jericho Scott." The glider sagged as he sat beside me.

I couldn't pretend I wasn't glad to see him. I had been sitting on the screen porch sipping iced tea and watching the neighborhood grow darker and darker when Shagg pulled into the driveway. I hadn't realized how the quiet intimidated me.

Shagg rocked gently, his long legs stretched in front of him. "I talked with Sudie," he said. "Didn't learn a lot; she met this Nelson guy at a wildlife lecture back in the spring, and they've been friends ever since."

"Just friends? What about Ralph?"

Shagg took a gulp of my tea. "I think ole Ralph's on his way out."

I nodded. "Sudie will have trouble with that. You know how she carries the guilt of the world on her shoulders. I'll bet her conscience is giving her fits."

He laughed. "We don't call her 'Saint Sudie' for nothing!"

• • •

I had no reason to be afraid after Shagg left. He had insisted on coming inside with me, checking every possible entrance, and I knew the police had stepped up their surveillance of Kennemore's Crossing. Besides, Jericho was right next door. "Call if you need me," he had said, and it was reassuring to look across at his lighted windows. If I stood on the back porch and listened carefully, I could hear the Beatles singing "Lucy in the Sky with Diamonds." They wrote music to make the soul dance a jig to heaven, he said, quoting somebody. I didn't care who; whatever Jericho Scott said sounded pretty good to me.

I thought of Miss Baby alone in that big old house with her nephew locked away in jail and decided to give her a call. She sounded glad to hear from me. "I was just thinking about you," she said. "I hope you're not alone."

"Shagg was here for a while," I told her. "I think he's adopted me." I waited for her to laugh but she didn't. "Are you all right, Miss Baby? Is there anything I can do?"

"Not now, dear, thank you. Things will work out in the long run." She sounded frail, hurt—like someone who couldn't defend herself. Like her name.

That nosy Florence Gilroy phoned as I was getting ready for bed. "Jane, is everything all right over there? I just couldn't go to sleep until I put myself at ease," she said. "Why, if anything should happen, your mother would never forgive me." I could just picture her standing there in her pink nylon nightie with cold cream on her face.

"Tried to catch you at the funeral," Florence went on, "but Jeanette and I went on to the cemetery . . . stifling up there, but I thought Brother Venable gave a right sweet little prayer. . . . Now, are you sure you're okay?"

"I think Sudie's coming by later," I lied. I smiled as I hung up the phone. Any means to an end, I told myself.

When the telephone rang again, I almost didn't answer, thinking it was Florence with a second installment. "Just to remind you I'm here," Jericho said. "And . . . it's midnight, and time passes, and I sleep alone."

"That makes two of us," I said, laughing. A pity, I thought.

I should have gone to sleep smiling. In spite of all my griping, it was good to know there were people who cared about Jane Cannon, all alone in the house at Kennemore's Crossing. And when Papa Sam found out I was here by myself, I would probably have hell to pay. I just didn't know I would pay so soon.

After what seemed like hours of slugging it out with my pillow, I finally fell asleep. But my sleep was filled with dreams: lethargic dreams of dark gray shadows and strange weeping trees. I stirred and drew my numb hand from beneath the pillow, rubbing it back to life. I felt empty, desolate, completely without hope. And in the deep, black stillness of the house, I cried.

Outside my door, in the hall that should have been empty, someone walked. Terror replaced despair as I clutched the covers about me and watched the door open slowly. A tall cloaked figure stood in the dim light with a basket on her arm. Her eyes had a cold yellow glow.

Chapter Ten

I jumped from the bed screaming, but the nightmare wouldn't go away. I felt ten years old again, and all the scary demons of an unsure world lurked just outside my door. Only this one was in the room with me; my parents weren't sleeping conveniently close by, and I was supposed to be old enough to take care of myself. I seized the first thing I touched in the dark—a framed photograph of my grandfather in his World War II uniform—and hurled it at the chilling silhouette. I heard the glass shatter as downstairs someone pounded on the door and shouted my name. When I turned on the light, the figure was gone, and the smashed picture lay facedown against the far wall. Papa Sam had come through for me again.

I was freezing by the time I reached the kitchen, and my hands shook so I could hardly unlock the door. For every dark shadow, each turn of the stairs, I expected the Widow Brumley to lunge at me, snatch me away with her cold, talonlike hands.

Jericho grabbed me to him, wrapped his arms around me. He wore nothing but gym shorts, but his body radiated warmth. I could have stayed there contentedly all night. "You're as cold as yesterday's coffee," he said. "Was it that man again? Where was he?"

I shook my head and forced myself to pull away. "It

was the widow—old Ma Brumley—she was going to kill me! I know she was!" I couldn't stop shivering. "Jericho, it was horrible. I've never been so scared in my life . . . and it was so dark. I felt like I was smothering."

He stroked my hair, my face. "A darkness which may be felt."

"Yes, how did you know?"

"I didn't; it's from the Bible—Exodus."

I saw something in his eyes: doubt? I wrapped myself in the closest thing at hand, which happened to be a clean towel from the laundry basket. "I *saw* her! Believe me, somebody was in my room!"

"What's this? What's going on here?" A disheveled Eulonia stationed herself in the doorway. "Was that you yelling bloody murder again? You must've scared ten years off my life!"

I wished it had been the last ten, then felt ashamed of myself. Eulonia was Eulonia, and she just couldn't help it. "Somebody was in my room," I said. "Somebody in a dark cloak . . . and with yellow eyes."

Eulonia smiled. "Yellow eyes, huh? Well, where'd he go? Up the chimney?"

If I ignore her, maybe she'll go away, I thought. "She has to be around here somewhere," I said to Jericho. "I'm sure all the doors and windows were locked."

I followed him through the rooms, one by one, flooding them with light, checking every closet and under every bed. No one was there.

"Sometimes dreams seem real," Eulonia said. "Especially bad dreams." She rubbed her bleary eyes and yawned. "And we all know you're not quite yourself after all that's happened."

What did she mean—*after all that's happened?* But Jericho spared me from answering. "I think we should call the police," he said.

"No!" I practically slammed my hand on his arm. "Please, not this time! It's no use. There's nothing here." I just couldn't face them again.

"Well, I'm going to try and get some sleep with what

little time I have left," Eulonia said. "Some of us have to be in early, you know." She paused on her way out. "Do you have anything to take? You know, something to relax you, help you settle down?"

Was the woman trying to tag me as a pill-popping neurotic? "Thanks, I'll be okay," I said, eager to see the last of her for a while. But I knew I wouldn't close my eyes again that night.

"Jane! Come here!" Jericho called from the living room. "Did you unlock the door to the screen porch?"

"No, I locked it behind me before I went up to bed." I stared at the familiar door as if it were malignant. "This must be how she got inside. But how? I'll swear that door was bolted!"

Jericho stepped outside and turned on the porch light. At the same time, I saw the kitchen light go on next door. I heard him gasp, and found him standing there, fixed, staring at the tile floor. "Wait! Don't come out here!" He held up a hand, but it was too late. I had already seen it: the spatter of blood at his feet.

The sprinkle of red led to the screen door—there was a smudge on the white paint above the handle—before the gory trail disappeared into the grass. "I don't care what you say," Jericho said as he led me back inside. "We're calling the police."

And then we heard Eulonia scream.

Like a ghastly apparition she ran toward us across the lawn. "Shelba Jean's gone! Oh my God, he's taken her— my baby! Help me, please—do something—before it's too late, before he kills her like the others."

"I don't blame Eulonia for being frantic," I told Shagg when he came by the store the next morning. "The girl's bed hadn't been slept in, and her car is still in the garage. Look, I know Shelba Jean Moody, and she'd never willingly leave that new Toyota!" I refolded a stack of tee shirts. "Police don't know what to think. It looks like she just walked off—or somebody took her."

Alice Boggs sighed. "Lord, I hope not. Poor Eulonia. They'll have to put her in a straitjacket."

"I think the doctor gave her something," I said. "Miss Baby's with her. I should've offered to stay, I guess, but Eulonia aggravates me more than anybody I know." I patted the soft knit shirts, smoothed them with my hand. "You know how she's always going on about how tired she is and overworked and how everybody takes advantage of her!"

Alice gently took my hand and led me from the shirt counter. "You've folded those things three times, Jane. You must be ready to drop. Why don't you go home and get some sleep?"

Because I'm afraid to close my eyes, I wanted to tell her. Sudie had called earlier and insisted I stay with her, and I didn't argue—yet I was in no hurry to sleep. Sleeping had made me vulnerable to whatever had happened the night before. I still wasn't sure it had been real.

Shagg stood beside me. "Jane, you locked that door. I remember checking it just before I left."

"Then somebody must have a key." I said it softly because it was too horrible to admit aloud.

"Did they find out where the blood came from?" Alice asked.

I shook my head. "Police took samples—and fingerprints, of course. I'm just glad it didn't come from me!"

"I think it was put there as a warning," Shagg said. "Somebody meant to scare you."

"But why?"

"You've been asking questions . . . seeing frizzy-haired phantoms, bearded men, old Ma Brumley . . . and dissecting Chloe's last column. You suspect everybody." Shagg took my cold hands and held them against his chest. "Looks like you've muddied somebody's water, Jane Cannon."

"I wonder what that column did mean?" I asked. "Miss Baby acted like that reference to her college reunion was a big joke. There wasn't any romance involved."

"Maybe not with that man, but there was somebody."

90

Alice rang up a sale and saw her customer on his way. "Don't forget, Baby Kennemore and I grew up in the same crowd, and she fell hard for some boy up there; only I think he ended up marrying somebody else."

Poor Miss Baby! Did she ever stop hurting? I looked up from the rack of blouses I was marking down. "Miss Baby says some of these kids at the high school are really into the occult, Shagg."

He shrugged. "Most teenagers are fascinated by the supernatural. Remember how we used to watch horror movies?"

"But this is different. It sounds like they have some kind of cult. I think they've been meeting in the woods for some time now."

Shagg raised my chin with a gentle finger. "Hey, I know these kids. Some of them get carried away sometimes, but not to the extent you're talking about. They're okay, Jane. Really."

"You don't think they had anything to do with Shelba Jean's disappearance?"

He frowned. "I don't know. . . . God, I hope not." He whirled around as Sudie threw open the door, breathless and red faced, as if she had run all the way.

"Have you heard? Somebody vandalized two cemeteries last night!" Sudie brushed past a rack of costume jewelry, knocking bracelets to the floor. "They had already dug several feet into the grave where Etta Lucas is buried before a patrol car scared them away." She scooped up the jewelry and tossed it onto the counter. "But they took whatever was left of some man buried out in the country."

I gripped the edge of the counter. "Who?"

"I don't know, and you wouldn't either," Sudie told me. "He died way back in the twenties. I guess they picked his grave because it was out of the way. Nobody uses that graveyard anymore."

"They're planning something tonight—it's part of their ritual, all this grisly business. Shelba Jean might already be dead." I looked around for Shagg, but he was on his way out. The door jingled on his leaving.

"What about that man they arrested?" Alice asked. "The one who had Chloe's extra key?"

"Dillard Moore? He's out on bail," Sudie said. "Been out since yesterday I heard."

"I wonder if he had anything to do with what happened to Shelba Jean? After all, they used to date." I frowned. It could have been a man dressed as the widow who had stood at the foot of my bed.

"I'm sure the police will check it out," Alice said. "And I imagine they'll be keeping an eye on the woods tonight, too."

I paced to the back of the store. "What kind of people are we dealing with here? Aren't you just the least bit curious? I've had it with these loonies!" I turned to face them. "Let's go out there tonight and see what happens! There's safety in numbers; let's *do* it—find out what's going on!"

"Are you crazy?" Sudie stared at me. "That's what police are for."

"And what have they done so far? It's been four months since Etta was killed, and as far as I know, they don't have a clue to who murdered Chloe!" I realized I was shouting. "Or why," I added quietly.

Alice took my hands in hers. "Just give them time— they'll get to the bottom of this. I know they will." She gave my fingers a squeeze. "Meanwhile, we don't need any more victims!"

I wanted to crawl into a corner and cry. Instead, I made myself smile. "Well, if we're going to be ready for that sale tomorrow, I guess we'd better get on with it."

Cannons' Clothing had run an ad in *The Sun* promoting our summer sale, and since part of the shipment we had been expecting didn't come in until that afternoon, Sudie pitched in and helped, staying long after Alice left that day. The two of us stopped only for sandwiches, which we ate on the back steps of the store.

"After your midnight visitor, I'm surprised your

grandpa hasn't called," Sudie said, crunching wax paper into a wad.

"Oh, he already has," I told her. "I think Papa Sam's upset with me. He thought I was staying with you last night." I slapped at a mosquito. "I wish I *had* been."

Sudie looked at me with her dark, solemn eyes. "Tell me about Jericho Scott."

I smiled. "He didn't dress up like the widow—and he didn't drip blood on my porch—if that's what you mean."

"How do you know he didn't?" Sudie sighed. "Oh, he seems nice enough, all right, but what do you really know?"

"Enough," I said. "I know enough." But I knew I was whistling in the dark.

"Now, about this Nelson Fain," I said as we went inside. "You're in love with him, aren't you?"

Sudie finger-dusted the ivy plant in the office window, one leaf at a time. "You're just not going to give up, are you?" She shrugged. "I've never felt this way about anybody. Not Ralph, not anybody. We didn't mean for it to happen. . . . It just did."

"Does Ralph know?"

"Not yet."

"Why not?"

Sudie shook her head. "I just couldn't think of a way—without hurting him, I mean. He'll never understand! I guess that's why I never set a wedding date. Something was missing. Ralph and I were never a set—a pair."

"And you and Nelson are?"

She threw back her head and smiled. "Yes!"

"He's not married, is he?"

Sudie looked at her watch. "Of course not. Look, will you be much longer? If I don't put a load in the wash, I won't have a thing to wear tomorrow."

"Probably less than an hour, but go on; if I see it's going to take longer, I'll call." I followed Sudie to the street. "Hey, you're not going to leave me hanging, are you? Tell me more about this mystery man."

"Jane, I can't. I've said too much already. Promise you won't say anything about this, okay?"

"But—"

"I mean it. It's important. Cross your heart?"

"Cross my heart," I said, and did.

I stood at the window as Sudie drove away. The skies were the color of dark smoke, and night would soon obscure whatever gruesome things were taking place in the Widow's Woods. I scanned the empty street where token lights gleamed from stores locked and deserted for the night. Even Fred O'Leary at the end of the block had put *The Sun* to bed, and the wide street was lit only by eerie blue white lamps overhead.

I hurriedly sorted the stack of children's play clothes remaining to be priced, eager to be out of my goldfish bowl on Main Street. Even though I couldn't see them, I was aware of the dark hills beyond town. The widow had spun her web well, and one by one, the people of the little town were being caught up in it.

Chapter Eleven

I munched a doughnut on the drive to town the next morning, searching on the radio for news of Shelba Jean, but according to the eight-thirty broadcast, she still remained missing. "Eulonia suspects the worst," Miss Baby had said when I talked with her the night before. "She's cleaning out closets; everything's piled on the floor. . . . No one can do a thing with her!"

I had to agree, it didn't look good. But what in the world did Chloe, Etta Lucas, and Shelba Jean Moody have in common—other than being female and living in the same town? Was there a connection somewhere? And what—if anything—had gone on in the Widow's Woods last night?

I didn't have to wait long to find out. Fred O'Leary sauntered in on the pretext of buying a tie soon after I opened the store.

He swung the rack around and studied a bright blue paisley. "Well, they slipped out on 'em again last night," Fred said, glancing up to see if I was listening.

I was. "Who slipped out?"

"That bunch out in the Widow's Woods—same ones who robbed that grave—that's who! Somebody must've warned them. By the time the police got there, every last one had up and vanished, just as quiet as you please, like they weren't ever there."

I searched for an eight and a half narrow in a plain white pump for a shoeless customer. "How do you know they were there?" I asked.

"Because they left Homer Boyd behind—or what was left of him."

"Homer Boyd?"

"Fellow whose grave was broken into out in Old Corinth Cemetery. Wasn't much left but a skull."

I could hear myself swallow. "Were you there?"

Fred held the tie under his chin and put it back. "Uh-huh; got there just after dark, but it was too late. I don't think we were too far behind them, though. We found a couple of black candle stubs. You could tell they left in a hurry."

"Do they know who it was?"

He shook his head. "If they do, they're not saying."

"I wonder if Dillard Moore had anything to do with it. He was out on bail the night Shelba Jean disappeared. But surely the police have looked into that."

"I reckon. But they haven't brought him back in, and they can't watch him every minute." Fred gave up on the ties and chose a plaid visored cap instead. "That boy's a wrong one, all right; don't know why Miss Baby puts up with him."

"Do you think she's afraid of him?"

"Could be." Fred pulled out a worn billfold and slowly parted with a frayed five dollar bill. "She wore her arm in a sling for a while back in the winter. Said she'd sprained her wrist, but I wouldn't be surprised if that Dillard had something to do with it."

"Your grandpa phoned," Alice said later that morning as I was trying to cram fat Mrs. Abercrombie into a size fourteen dress. "Said he'd see you later."

I gave the zipper a jerk. It didn't budge. "Is that all? Does he want me to call him back?"

Alice shrugged. "Nope. That's all he said."

Still mad, I thought, peeling the dress off my customer. I would have to make it up to him—and I knew just how to do it. I'll take him a pecan pie, I decided; that was his favorite, and the small bakery in the shopping center made the best I'd ever tasted. They were expensive, but they were worth it. I smiled. Oh, well, peace at any price. And while I was at it, I'd get one for Eulonia as well.

But my grandfather's car was not in his garage when I stopped by after work, and there was no sign of Mrs. Lovejoy. The front door was locked, but I knew where Papa Sam kept an extra key to the back door, so I tucked the bakery box under my arm and walked around the house. The pie was still warm and it smelled wonderful. I would leave it on the kitchen table, but not until I had tried just one tiny little piece.

In the lengthening afternoon shadows, I almost didn't see the circled pentagram drawn in the dust beside the steps. And my grandfather's heirloom sword was thrust upright in the middle of it!

"It had dried blood all over the blade!" I shuddered. "How do I know it wasn't Papa Sam's blood? Or Shelba Jean's?" Jericho and I sat by the pond in the town park, watching the fading sunset in the water. Behind us a family grilled hamburgers, and although they smelled wonderful, I wasn't hungry. I tossed a pebble into the still green water and watched the ripple of circles. My life seemed to be going in circles as well.

"The police seem to think your grandfather's all right," Jericho said. "His car is gone, and he did call you earlier."

"But why? Where would he go? He always lets somebody know if he's going on one of his fishing trips, and he didn't take any of his usual gear." I wanted to put my head down and cry, but I knew it wouldn't do any good. My forehead ached and my eyes burned. If only I had taken the time to return his call that morning. And the sword. I wished I could close my eyes and erase the memory of it. This time I threw a bigger rock, jumping back to

97

avoid the splash. If I could find the person who had drawn that hideous diagram, I'd like to shove him in, too.

I let Jericho lead me around the edge of the pond, feeling like a shaky invalid who needed a strong arm. "I wonder if it was Nathan Lovejoy?" I said. "And why did he return the sword like that? It's cruel!"

He took my hand. "The police have the sword now; maybe they'll find some prints. I wouldn't be surprised if the blood turned out to be like the other."

I hoped it would. The blood samples taken from our porch had come from a chicken, we learned; and the only fingerprints they found were made by friends and family members. Whoever was causing all the trouble knew enough to wear gloves, or else it was someone I knew.

"Let's go somewhere we can talk," Jericho suggested, steering me up the steps to the street. "I'll think a lot clearer on barbecue and beer."

The drive to the restaurant relaxed me, and when I settled across from him in the high-backed pine booth, I was glad I had agreed to come. The beer was cold and good, and the smell of hickory smoke permeated the dim, paneled room.

Jericho drank deeply from his frosty stein and sighed. "Now, what about your grandfather's housekeeper? Does she have any idea where he is?"

I traced a knothole in the tabletop. "She hasn't seen him since yesterday; he left her a note to feed the cat. Mrs. Lovejoy has her own key."

He frowned. "And his friend . . . what's that you called him?"

"Cooter. Cooter Edwards. I can't find him, either. Nobody answers the phone."

"Maybe your grandfather left word with Sudie. Have you talked with her?"

I shook my head. "She's out running around somewhere, probably with that Nelson Fain. Sudie's seeing an awful lot of him," I confided. "And she doesn't know a thing about him, except he's an expert on birds."

Jericho sat back and looked at me. "Don't be too sure,

Jane. Your friend is a big girl now. I expect she knows what she wants." I could tell he was trying not to laugh.

I tried to look away, but his dark eyes held me. What did he mean by that? That I—Jane—didn't? Yet I had to admit to myself it was true—always had been. I *didn't* know what I wanted. Life had always been hit or miss with me, even my engagement to Mac. Since our parents were close friends, we had always seen a lot of each other; I guess you could say our relationship was sort of *there.* And that suited me just fine. Mac McCullough was good-looking, intelligent, and ambitious, and when he kissed me, the fire went down to my toes. Why look further? But after Mac started medical school, all he wanted to discuss were his classes, his friends, and himself, while I took off in an entirely different direction with my own interests. We really had grown apart. I wondered how long the marriage would have lasted if my fiancé hadn't had the good sense to call it off. I sat up straighter. I had become conveniently accustomed to someone else telling me what to do. Well, I was tired of it.

"Other than the obvious," I said later over coffee, "I can't see any connection between the two murder victims and Shelba Jean."

"Maybe they knew some of the same people?" he suggested.

I sighed. It was apparent he hadn't been raised in a small town. "In Sweetsprings," I explained, "everybody knows everybody."

"More than just that. Think about close friends, relatives, co-workers—neighbors."

"Well, there's Miss Baby and her nephew," I said.

Jericho sipped his coffee. "Aren't you forgetting somebody?"

"Who?" I laughed. "Oh! Well, there's me." Slowly I stirred sugar into my cup. "Miss Baby used to play bridge some with Chloe," I said. "And I'm sure she taught both girls." I frowned. "And then there's Dillard Moore. He dated Shelba Jean awhile, and I'm sure he must have known Chloe—especially if he was over there much."

Jericho looked up at me. "If rumors are true, he was seeing the Lucas girl, too."

"Where did you hear that?"

He counted on his fingers. "Let's see . . . gas station, barber shop, the plumber who worked on my shower—need any more sources?"

"He scares me," I admitted. "I don't like having him around. Why doesn't Miss Baby throw the creep out?"

"I don't think she can." Jericho lowered his voice. "From what I overheard of an argument the other day, it seems like Miss Baby doesn't really own that place."

"What?" I set my mug down so hard the coffee sloshed onto the table.

"When her mother died the house went to her older sister—Dillard's mother—with the stipulation that Miss Baby live there as long as she liked, but she has to struggle to keep it up. I don't think her sister gives her much money, and that big old place just slurps up what little she has. Think how much it costs her to keep up that pool even part of the summer."

"How do you know this?" My voice sounded unusually loud, and I looked around to see if I had attracted attention, but no one seemed to care.

"The two of them were in the orchard and I was on the other side of the hedge, fertilizing the azaleas. She was trying to get him to help with some painting, repairs around the house, but he wouldn't have any part of it. Told her he didn't care if the whole damn house fell in, and as soon as she died he was going to sell it anyway!"

I couldn't speak for the awfulness of it. Poor Miss Baby! And to think I had passed notes all through her Latin classes. I had noticed that the big house seemed shabby, but my neighbor had always been eccentric. I just thought her mind was on higher things. It would be impossible to keep up a place like that on a teacher's pay.

I reached across to Jericho. "I've got to know," I said.

He smiled. "Humor me. What?"

"I have to know where that slime Dillard Moore was

when Shelba Jean disappeared. And whether they've found her or not. Do you think the police will tell us?"

"There's one way to find out," he said. "Got a quarter for the phone?"

But the officer in charge was noncommittal, admitting only that they were aware of the relationships between Dillard Moore and the two girls. "Besides," he confided, "the Moore guy has an alibi: A friend of his got married the night Shelba Jean Moody disappeared, and he was in the wedding."

"Are you staying with Sudie again tonight?" Jericho asked later as we turned into Kennemore's Crossing. I had left my car with extra clothes in the driveway, and was glad I wouldn't have to go inside. The house looked dark and threatening, and I wished I had thought to leave a porch light burning.

I smiled. Was it my imagination, or had he sounded wistful? "I promised Papa Sam," I said. "Besides, after the other night, I'm not too crazy about staying here alone."

Next door at Eulonia's a lamp glowed in the living room window—like a beacon, I thought. And then I remembered the pie. "Do you think it's too late to see Eulonia?" I asked, half hoping he would say yes. "I've been browbeating myself all day for turning my back on her."

"Why not? Doesn't look like she's asleep."

Eulonia met us at the door. There were food stains down the front of her dress, and her hair looked as if it hadn't been combed all day. She stood in the doorway with her feet planted firmly apart, as if we were going to storm the threshold and try to sell her a vacuum cleaner. I held out the box of pastry, relieved that we weren't invited in. "I've been thinking about you, Eulonia. I'm sorry . . . I wish there were something I could do." To my extreme agitation I was getting teary-eyed and I looked to Jericho for help. He stood there like a wooden Indian.

Eulonia wasn't wearing her glasses and her eyes looked weak and red. She nodded solemnly and accepted the pie.

"Thank you. I'd ask you in, but it's late, and I didn't sleep a wink last night."

I backed away, muttering soothing phrases to the door as it closed in my face. I wasn't doing a very good job of this, but at least I had made an effort. As we stepped off the porch, I noticed that Chloe's geraniums were dying for lack of water. "Well," I said aloud. "At least I can do that much."

Jericho sat patiently on Eulonia's steps while I gave each plant a much-needed drink from a watering can I found in the tool shed. I was aware that my neighbor probably didn't care if the flowers died or not, but Chloe would have cared, so I did it for Chloe.

"You're not planning to water the whole yard, are you?" Jericho asked as I saturated the last begonia. I started to reply when an outside door opened on Chloe's side of the house and Eulonia spoke in a harsh whisper.

". . . beside myself with worry . . . just tell me she's all right!"

Jericho quietly pulled me back into the shadows while a man spoke in low, threatening tones. I couldn't distinguish his words.

". . . all I have . . . if anything happens . . ." Eulonia was crying.

I strained to hear the man's muttered answer, but a passing truck drowned his words.

"I'll give you anything!" Eulonia promised. "Only for God's sake, please bring my baby home!"

I felt the pressure of Jericho's hand on my arm. "It's the man who took Shelba Jean!" I whispered. "It has to be!" I wanted to move closer, get a better look at his face, but Jericho held me back as we heard the man's heavy footsteps plodding toward us through the dry grass. Seconds later, as we huddled against the porch banisters, the bushy-haired man emerged pushing a motorcycle and humming his favorite hymn.

Chapter Twelve

I wanted to throw myself upon him, pound him into the ground. This was in all likelihood the man who had kidnapped Shelba Jean and killed the other two women as well . . . and he had the nerve to hum "Rock of Ages," just as if he were sitting up in the choir or something! My one last fingernail bit into my flesh, but I didn't even feel it. I stood stiffly, listening to myself breathe, and watched the man ride away—a black silhouette against the gray night. And inside the house, Eulonia wept.

"Hurry! We have to follow him!" I started to run for the car, then paused. "Somebody should phone the police."

But Jericho lagged behind, examining the palm of his hand. "Hold on! It's not that simple. It sounds like Eulonia made a deal with this guy. If we bring police in now, there's no telling what he might do." He blew on his hand and shook it. "I wish you'd trim that nail. You almost clawed a hole in my hand."

I gulped. No wonder I hadn't felt it! "Sorry! But, Jericho, what if we lose track of this man? We might never know who he is or what he's done with that girl."

He walked with me across the lawn. "His name is Elias Hawkins, and he lives in that trailer park just past the brickyard."

"How do you know that?"

Jericho traced the line of my jaw with one finger. "Let's just say I've done a little research of my own."

"But he may be holding Shelba Jean—he might have killed her!"

He shook his head. "I'm not saying he doesn't know where she is, but Shelba Jean Moody's not in that trailer, Jane—dead or alive. If we don't know any more in a day or so, it's time to tell the police, but I don't want to be responsible for the consequences if we blow this thing too soon. Do you?" His fingers moved to the nape of my neck.

I didn't want to be anything but kissed, and I was. In spite of what had happened, those last few moments with Jericho made me feel desirable again, exciting. Yet some peculiar instinct told me we were being watched the whole time.

The next day the feeling remained. I spent the morning at the store, met Sudie for lunch, and afterward the two of us stopped by Papa Sam's. I didn't want to go inside alone, and hoped to see my grandpa's familiar tan Dodge back in its usual place. But the garage was still empty, and the ugly, threatening pentagram etched into the dry soil was the only sign that all was not as it should be.

Sudie frowned when she saw it. "I've seen that before; it's one of those symbols the kids like to draw—has something to do with Satan worship."

I scuffed the drawing with my foot. "What does a star in a circle have to do with the devil?"

"It's a five-pointed star," Sudie explained. "They believe there's power in the number five. And see . . . if these two points here are ascending, they stand for the horns of the devil. They represent evil."

"Ugh!" I smeared what was left of the sketch until my shoes were pink with a fine layer of dust. "And kids in *junior high* are into this?"

"Some of them. They're fascinated by it—like to read about it and listen to certain kinds of music. And they'll copy those symbols: pentagrams, swastikas—even inverted crosses on notebooks and things. I've seen them on the bathroom walls."

"Was Etta Lucas one of them?" I asked.

"I'm not sure," Sudie said. "She was in junior high before I taught there, you know. It's hard to know who's really into this stuff. Some of them just think it's fun—like we did when we used to tell ghost stories. They don't take it seriously." She looked away. "At least most of them don't."

"Did Shelba Jean?"

"Maybe. She'd be a likely candidate, but I never taught Shelba Jean. She was in that same class with Etta—in fact, I think they were pretty good friends."

"Etta Lucas!" I remembered her at eight with a room full of stuffed animals, and how excited she had been at her first ballet recital—all dressed up in a pink tutu and sequined tiara. "She didn't seem Shelba Jean's type."

"She got into kind of a wild crowd; I don't think Etta's parents liked her choice of friends. They sent her to stay with an aunt in Columbia last Christmas—to get her away, I guess. Obviously it didn't do any good."

"What do you mean?"

Sudie turned and looked at me. "Why, didn't you know? Etta was almost two months pregnant when she died."

I gave the brick-red earth a final kick. "No, I didn't know. What about the father? Was it Dillard Moore?"

She shrugged. "Maybe. Maybe not; he wasn't the only one from what I've heard. Etta matured too early for her own good, I'm afraid."

"And where was Dillard when she was killed?" Surely there hadn't been another convenient wedding.

"He was in some kind of automotive class over at the technical school. His instructor backs him up."

But it was only a few miles from the campus to the place where Etta died. How long would it take for him to slip away?

We quickly explored my grandfather's quiet house, looking for any clue to his whereabouts. Mrs. Lovejoy had left baked ham and candied sweet potatoes in the refrigerator for his dinner, but the food hadn't been touched. Looking at it, I felt a slash of cold and an over-powering urge to get out in the sun. I couldn't shed the image of Etta Lucas the last time I had seen her. She must have been twelve or thirteen wearing a baggy shirt and jeans, biking through town with that little dog in the basket. I hurried to the car.

"What was that?" I stopped suddenly. A shadow moved in the small grove of trees at the side of the house, and somewhere a twig snapped.

"What was what? I didn't hear anything."

"I thought I saw something," I said. "Guess I'm getting jumpy." I looked back as we pulled out of the driveway. Was someone standing just inside Papa Sam's garage, or was I seeing phantoms? I wished I hadn't promised Jericho not to tell about Eulonia's threatening visitor. I would have felt much better if I could spread around some of my doubts.

I told him that when I saw him later that afternoon. I also told him about Etta Lucas being pregnant.

"I don't mean to make you nervous, but this whole thing seems to center on your neighborhood," he said. "Especially Eulonia's place." He thought for a minute. "Dillard Moore is originally from Columbia, and Etta's parents sent her there last summer. What about Chloe? Did she ever live anywhere else?"

"Chloe was married for a while," I said. "I'd almost forgotten about that. It didn't work out. He was quite a bit older than she was, I think."

"When was this?"

"Back when I first started high school. He had something to do with the university."

"And Applegate's her maiden name?"

"Right. I don't think they were married but a year or so. And when Chloe came back to Sweetsprings, she moved in next door."

He nodded. "But for at least a year Chloe Applegate lived in Columbia. What about Eulonia?"

I told him about the little town near the coast. "I think she still has a cousin living there," I said. "But as far as I know, Eulonia's never lived in Columbia—probably never even been there."

Jericho grinned. "How about a little side trip?" he asked.

I leaned back against the seat of the gleaming little car and watched the land grow sandier and flatter as we drove from the Piedmont into the Sandhills section of the state. We left Sweetsprings about mid afternoon, and had over a two-hour drive ahead of us, but there was still a lot of daylight left.

"I don't suppose Cooter's heard from your grandfather?" Jericho asked, merging with the traffic on the busy highway.

"Don't know. Can't seem to catch him at home. Leola—that's his wife—said he hadn't gone with Papa Sam and she wasn't aware of any fishing trip." I swept the heavy hair from my neck and let the air conditioner do its job. "I don't know what's happened to everybody. Papa Sam's gone off to who knows where, and Sudie's fallen in love with a burglar."

He laughed. "What are you talking about?"

I told him how the man I had seen in Chloe's side of the house had resembled Nelson Fain. "That's why I wasn't convinced it was Dillard Moore. And I saw that same man with Chloe Applegate not long before she was killed!"

"Obviously Sudie has a few secrets, Jane."

"I guess so. But she's always been so predictable! Made good grades in school, practiced her music every day, and never, never got into trouble. That's why Shagg calls her 'Saint Sudie.' "

Jericho laughed. "A nickname is the hardest stone the devil can throw! I'd think she'd be more than ready for a change."

We stopped at the edge of the small city of Florence and treated ourselves to ice cream, which melted almost as fast as we could eat it. "Pity we didn't bring our suits," I said. "We're not that far from the beach." It would have been wonderful to wade into the green surf and let the waves splash away my worries.

Jerricho crunched the rest of his cone. "And we're not that far from Mullins, either. What was Eulonia's cousin's name again?"

"Myra . . . something. Updyke! Myra Updyke."

Jericho looked at me and smiled. "Wouldn't you like to pay her a visit?"

"I'll go anywhere as long as it's air-conditioned," I said.

At a convenience store on the outskirts of the little town, Jericho stopped at a phone booth. "There's still an Updyke over on Aiken Street," he said, flipping through the small directory. "Shall I call or you?"

I took a step backward. "You, by all means. I'm a terrible liar." I listened while he explained to the person on the other end of the line that he and his associate represented a publishing company that specialized in church cookbooks, and that her cousin in Sweetsprings had referred them to her. I shook my head at his obvious blarney. I wouldn't have believed him for a second.

But Myra Updyke did. Jericho smiled as he hung up. "Let's go! She only lives three blocks away."

Chapter Thirteen

Eulonia's Cousin Myra met us at the door of her neat brick home in a block of similar neat brick homes. The mailbox out front had geese stenciled on it, and a flock of wooden poultry paraded across the lawn. The cast-iron boot scraper at the front door was in the shape of a terrier, and after I saw the inside of Myra's gleaming home, I was surprised we weren't asked to use it.

"And how is Eulonia? My goodness, I haven't heard from her in years," Myra told us over a glass of tea. "I'm afraid the poor thing's had a right hard life. She married late, you know, and little Shelba Jean wasn't much more than a baby when Aaron was killed."

Jericho swirled the amber liquid in his glass. "How did it happen?"

"Construction accident," Myra Updyke said. "He worked for a demolition company, and there was an explosion in the old mill they were tearing down. Building burned for a week!"

"How awful!" I felt sorry (sort of) for all the times I had criticized our neighbor. "Did they . . . how did they—?"

"Oh, they got him out before the fire reached him," the woman said. "Still, it was pretty bad. He didn't even live long enough to get to the hospital."

My stomach felt peculiar. I was sorry I had eaten the ice cream. "Poor Eulonia. What a terrible way to remember someone you love."

Myra spoke softly. "I know. I tried to keep her away, but you know Eulonia—she had to see him for herself. I suppose we both did." Her faded blue eyes filled with tears. "I wish to the Lord I hadn't."

"I feel rotten," I said as we left Eulonia's cousin Myra waving good-bye at the door. "She really thinks we'll get in touch with her about that cookbook."

Jericho reached for my hand. "Don't worry; somebody will. I have a friend who knows someone in the business, and I'll pass the information along. Maybe I'll even get a commission!"

Still, I felt guilty about deceiving the woman, and I wasn't sure the information we had gained was worth the effort.

According to Myra Updyke, Eulonia had always lived in or near the little tobacco town of Mullins until she moved to Sweetsprings and next door to us. She didn't mention her ever spending time in Columbia.

"I'm so glad Eulonia has someone sharing that house," the woman had said. "Aaron didn't leave her much, you know, and I'm sure she can use the money, what with that child to educate and all."

This time I outwaited Jericho Scott. I didn't have the heart to tell Myra Updyke about Chloe's death and Shelba Jean's disappearance.

"You will let me know if you learn anything more?" Mrs. Updyke said after Jericho reluctantly told her what had been happening. Shaking her head, she followed us to the door. "I'm ashamed of myself for losing track—my own cousin! I'll call Eulonia tonight!"

The sun was still bright when we left Mullins behind and started home, and I was glad to close my eyes and let Jericho worry about the traffic.

"Here's that fish camp everybody's been talking about," Jericho said, turning into a restaurant a few miles out of town. "Let's give it a try. Deceit makes me hungry!"

110

Just about anything makes me hungry, but I wasn't going to admit it to him, and from all the cars in the parking lot, it looked as if we'd come to the right place.

"Look at that dark blue Ford turning in behind us," Jericho whispered as we started inside. "That guy's been following us all afternoon."

"Are you sure? I haven't noticed anybody." Shading my eyes with my hand, I tried to get a look at the driver, but the car disappeared around the side of the building. "There aren't that many good places to eat along this stretch of the road," I said. "It's probably just somebody going out for dinner."

Jericho wasn't convinced. "I'll swear that's the same car I saw when we turned off Mrs. Updyke's street back in Mullins."

But I had already caught a whiff of fresh fish, fried light and golden, and my stomach demanded something more substantial than the aroma that greeted us. I could already taste the crisp, oniony hush puppies and mounds of zippy slaw they always served on the side. I hurried inside the dim, air-cooled dining room with a smile of anticipation and almost collided with my ex-fiancé and his new girlfriend!

If a smile can slide, mine did. It did a vertical dive clear to my toes and oozed away somewhere between the cracks in the wide plank floor.

My dear Mac did a double take (well, actually, it was more like a triple take); and introduced his square-haired darling while performing an odd little jig toward the door. Bonnie Lynne, I noticed, had bony shoulders, a slight case of sunburn, and a bosom even smaller than mine. I had hoped for warts.

I thanked my Creator a thousand times for the good-looking man beside me with a slightly possessive hand on my arm, and did a fair job of how do you dos. It wasn't until they had left and the two of us were seated that I broke into uncontrollable giggling.

Of course I had to explain the situation to Jericho, who racked up even more points in his favor when he declared in outraged tones that Mac McCullough must be a complete fool and blind to boot. I agreed. Why, the woman had absolutely no rear end at all. She looked like a paper doll.

I didn't want to think about what I would look like after eating all that fried food, but it tasted even better than it smelled, and I'm afraid I cleaned my plate. We had both forgotten about the suspicious blue Ford until we finished our meal and stepped outside into the darkening parking lot.

"Guess who's still here?" Jericho said, unlocking the door to his car.

"Maybe they're having dessert." I felt full and contented—and even a little smug that my confrontation with Mac hadn't bothered me any more than it had. I had fully expected to hate Bonnie Lynne at first sight, but I hadn't. Of course, I wasn't crazy about her, either. Anyway, the person in the blue Ford wasn't high on my list of concerns, and I didn't mean for it to ruin what was left of my day.

I was relieved to see Sudie's car in our driveway when we reached home, but Eulonia's house looked lonely and sad, and I noticed a couple of ladies from her church whispering together as they left. "They act like Shelba Jean is already dead," I told Jericho. "Do you think she is?"

"I don't have the answers, Jane. I wish I did."

"But you have some of them, don't you? Why wouldn't you let me call the police when we saw that man with the motorcycle? How do you know he hasn't killed her by now?"

"He's being watched, Jane. Let's just leave it at that—okay?"

"No, it's not okay! How do you know that? Who's watching him?" He started to get out of the car, but I put a hand on his arm. "Wait a minute. Just who are you? Why are you here?"

Slowly he covered my hand with his, then brought it to his lips and kissed it before returning it to my lap. Then, very deliberately, he walked around to my side of the car. I was so caught up in the confusion of the moment I couldn't think of a thing to say.

"Jane, what does Cooter Edwards look like?" Jericho asked as we started inside.

I frowned. "Look, you're not getting away with evading one question by asking another."

"No, I mean it." He lowered his voice. "About how old is he?"

"About seventy, I guess . . . tall and lanky . . . wears an old straw hat that must've belonged to his grand-daddy. Why?"

"He's on the other side of that front wall. I saw him when we turned into your drive," Jericho whispered. "He's the guy in the blue Ford."

I looked up. "Who? Coo—"

"Shh! He's just over there. Watching us."

I sat down on the steps to laugh. I was so accustomed to seeing my grandfather's friend on foot, I had forgotten what kind of car he drove. I still didn't know where Papa Sam was, but he had left a bodyguard behind!

Monday morning he was still on duty. I sensed him behind me as I walked to the post office, but every time I looked around, Cooter ducked out of sight. I saw the yellowed crown of his hat poking above the fertilizer display in front of the hardware store; the worn brown tips of his shoes jutted from behind the gas pump at the corner filling station. He had haunted me like a specter the day before, sitting behind me in church and driving past my house at half-hour intervals. When did the man find time to eat and sleep? I smiled, planning how I would give him the slip.

"What on earth is that fool, Cooter Edwards, sneaking around behind you for?" Florence Gilroy paused in her stamp-licking and waylaid me with a sinewy hand. "He looks like an ostrich with the bends. And where's your granddaddy gotten off to? I've been trying to call him for three days now." She slammed a stamp with a mighty whack of her fist. "You're not stayin' by yourself, are you?

113

Why, I told Jeanette this morning, it's a wonder we don't all wake up dead with this grisly business going on!" With one hand clamped to my shoulder, she trailed after me to the stamp window. *"Digging up dead people!* Why, I never heard of such a thing. It's all this television and nasty movies. I said to Jeanette—"

It took at least five minutes to convince her that I was in no immediate danger of being abducted by either the evil grave-robbing cult or the sinister Cooter Edwards, and another five to pry myself loose. I leaned on the table for support as Florence marched away. I felt as if I had just donated a quart of blood.

"Hey, whatever it is, it can't be that bad . . . can it?"

I looked up into Shagg's freckled face. *"You!"* I poked a finger at his chest. "I've a few bones to pick with you."

He made a face. "Not the best choice of words—considering what's been going on."

"Never mind that." I took him by the arm, noticing that he had just collected mail from his box. "I thought you were going to have a serious talk with Sudie. She won't even listen to me."

"What do you mean?" He glanced at a couple of bills and stuffed them into his back pocket, then frowned at the handwriting on the third letter.

"You know very well what I mean. She and that Nelson Fain are as thick as honey, and I know he's hiding something. Shagg, I'm sure he knew Chloe!"

His blue eyes shimmered with concern. "We all knew Chloe, Jane; and I *did* talk with Sudie. It's not a bad thing to fall in love, you know . . . as long as it's with the right person." Shagg gave me one of his little puzzled smiles and slit open the envelope with his thumb. "My God, what's this?"

I watched him read the small folded note inside. His expression was about the same as when the Purvis brothers, Hoss and Moose, found out he'd propositioned their sister back in high school.

"What is it, Shagg? What's wrong?"

"Nothing! Somebody's idea of a joke, that's all." His hand shook as he shoved the message back inside.

He quickly folded the envelope before I could get a look at the handwriting, then watched in apparent dismay as a bright tatter of orange paper fluttered to the floor. I reached down and snatched it. It was a fragment of wrapping from a package of tangerine Lifesavers.

"You're in some kind of trouble, aren't you?" I shoved him outside and propelled him all the way down the street to the drugstore, ignoring the tall lanky shadow that trailed after us. "What's going on, Shagg? Tell me about it." We sat at a small table in the rear of the store, sipping Coke with crushed ice. I was glad Eulonia wasn't there to eavesdrop.

He stirred his drink with a straw. "There's nothing to tell. Really."

"Does it have anything to do with all this business in the Widow's Woods?"

Shagg looked up. "What do you mean?"

"What do you think I mean? Are you involved in Shelba Jean Moody's disappearance?"

He took a deep breath and looked at me. "Of course not!"

I felt relief melt through me. I thought he was telling the truth. "Tell me about Etta Lucas," I said. "Who did she run around with?"

Shagg shook ice into his mouth. "Oh, lord, Jane! Why ask me? I don't know."

"Yes, you do. Now, tell me!"

"Well . . . there was Kristabelle Douglas for one . . . and I saw her some with the Lovejoy kid."

"Nathan? Ruby's grandson Nathan? Who else?" I put my hand on his and felt his fingers curl over my palm. "What about Shelba Jean Moody?"

He shrugged. "Maybe. I guess so."

"Sudie said Etta was pregnant. Was Dillard Moore the father?"

"That's what they say. My God, Jane! Why are you asking me this?"

115

"Because I have to know." I squeezed his fingers. "Shagg, did any of them belong to this Satan-worshipping group?"

He pushed back his chair and leaned over me. "I can't tell you what I don't know, Jane." He caught my hand briefly as he walked past. "Just be careful—please."

I sat there looking after him. "Be careful of what?" I asked. But he was gone.

I walked slowly past Cooter Edwards who, with his back to me, pretended to be looking at greeting cards. "I'm leaving now, Mr. Edwards!" I called, letting the door swing shut behind me.

Alice Boggs was straightening the sale table when I got back to the store. "That sergeant from the police department called," she said. "They've analyzed the blood on that sword."

Absently I picked up a pair of sheer underpants and ran them through my fingers. I didn't want to hear this. Why hadn't I just kept on walking until I was far away from this town? Far away from the Widow's Woods and the dark secrets it held?

"It was human blood," Alice went on. "A positive—the same type as Shelba Jean Moody's."

Chapter Fourteen

Did Eulonia know about the blood on the sword? I watched the house next door as I mopped the kitchen, expecting to hear hysterical crying—or worse—but the gray-trimmed house could have been empty for all that went on there. I swirled sudsy water underneath the table, working my way to the other side of the room. There was satisfaction in physical labor, and I was ready to take on the bushy-haired man himself if I had to! I tossed the dirty water out back, glancing at the adjoining yard. I couldn't see Twin Towers, but Jericho's windows were dark, and the whole area seemed to be in a deep sleep. Maybe Eulonia was asleep, too, I thought.

Business had been slow since the sale, and I had left the store a little early to take care of things at home. I was glad I did. Soon after I arrived, my parents called from a small Yorkshire village to leave a number where I could reach them. They were on their way to a long-awaited tour of northern England and the Lake Country, and sounded so young and eager that I couldn't bear to tell them about Chloe and Shelba Jean. "I'm fine," I said, eyeing a scattering of crumbs on the kitchen counter and unwashed breakfast dishes in the sink. "The house is fine . . . and Papa Sam sends love." Or he would, I thought, if he were here.

The house smelled stale and musty, and dust had begun to accumulate on my mother's dark furniture. I threw open the windows and felt my spirits lift with the gloom as sunlight invaded the house once more and the long, cherry dining table gleamed with the lemony scent of polish. I snipped three yellow roses for the kitchen. I would be eating alone tonight, but there was no reason I couldn't dine in some semblance of style. The roses reminded me of Chloe; and like Chloe, they would lend their special charm for a brief period and then be gone. One by one I stuck them into a vase. With all my deductions, I still had no idea who had killed my neighbor or what had happened to Shelba Jean. And I was really getting worried about Papa Sam! Even Cooter claimed he didn't know where he was, and I had no reason to doubt him.

I started a new mystery book while I sat down to salad and a sandwich. Sudie would be having dinner with Nelson. (She hadn't admitted as much—just said she'd be going out, but I knew that one and one didn't add up to Ralph.) And Jericho Scott . . . well, I had no idea where he was.

"I should be in before too late," Sudie had promised when she called. "You sure you'll be all right there alone?"

I laughed. "With big bad Cooter on guard? Never fear!" Still, I was glad Jericho had insisted on installing new locks since the night of the "Widow's" visit.

I crunched on a potato chip. Cooter was out on the screen porch now; I could hear the glider squeaking. I had tried without success to get him to either go home or come inside and join me, but Cooter had been given his orders and was not one to be easily swayed. He was fine, he said, and had already eaten, although he just might be tempted to try one of those nice sandwiches and a glass of tea—and maybe a cookie if I had one to spare.

I was upstairs making the bed for Sudie when I saw Jericho's lights go on next door, and soon the sentimental words of "Yesterday" reached me through the open window. He had planned to work on his novel tonight, he said, so I wasn't expecting him to drop by, and was surprised an hour or so later when someone rang the doorbell.

Thinking it was Mr. Edwards, I hurried downstairs, but there was no one at the door, and from the screen porch came the distinctive sounds of snoring. I could still hear music from Jericho's stereo across the lawn. Then who had rung the bell? I was beginning to get a little jittery as I glanced through the window. The front stoop was deserted, but a folded paper lay on the welcome mat.

On plain unlined paper someone had printed: IF YOU WANT TO KNOW WHERE YOUR GRANDFATHER IS, COME TO THE WIDOW'S WOODS TONIGHT! I crumpled the note in my hand and started to throw it away, then thought better of it. What would Papa Sam be doing in the Widow's Woods, and what was I expected to do about it? If this was a joke it wasn't funny! I tucked the message in the pocket of my shorts. Jericho would know.

I skirted the pool where Chloe had died, grateful for the dark wall that hid it, and ran through the small orchard where hard, green apples clung. The Beatles had switched to a different tune when I knocked at the door of the carriage house, and a light burned inside, but no one answered my pounding. Probably can't hear over all this noise, I thought, jabbing in irritation at the bell. Still no Jericho.

"Hey! Anybody home?" I pushed open the door and stepped inside. The room appeared to be empty, although a typewriter with paper in it sat on a desk in the corner, and the Beatles now sang of a yellow submarine. I peeked into the tiny kitchen, the sparsely furnished bedroom where books leaned in towering stacks beside the bed, then I circled the quarters once more before the truth slapped me in the face: *Jericho Scott wasn't there, but he had wanted me—or someone—to believe he was!* I flipped off the switch on the stereo. If I never heard the Beatles again, it would be too soon! On the sheet of paper in the typewriter a repeated sentence filled the page: *Now is the time for all good men to come to the aid of their country.* No wonder he wouldn't let me read his novel! It was a little weak on plot.

I stood at the window. The space where Jericho had parked his car was empty. How long had he been gone? I felt excluded, betrayed, as if everyone except Jane Cannon shared some deep, dark secret. Was I not to be trusted? Is this how paranoia began?

I slammed the door on my way out, almost stumbling in my eagerness to get away: away from Jericho and the grim house next door, away from my sleeping "watch dog" on the porch. Was Jericho trying to keep me from finding out something? But what? And why was he pretending to write a book? I thought of his fondness for spouting quotations. Well, I could quote a few verses, too! Unfortunately they all had to do with snakes. Lines from Milton I had learned in college burned in my memory— something to do with the serpent deceiving Eve. The snake was male, of course. I stood in the dark and breathed blackness. Even the air was bitter. I would go to the Widow's Woods, and I would go alone.

Taking time only to change into long pants, I eased my car out of the dark driveway. I would have to be self-reliant now. There was no one I could trust. Papa Sam was gone, and my assigned bodyguard had zonked out for the night. My best friend was out running around with her newfound love (who was in all likelihood a criminal), and Shagg was up to his eyeballs in some kind of trouble himself.

A sudden shower speckled the windshield as I turned onto the narrow two-lane road to the woods, and I was glad I'd left my raincoat in the car. The countryside seemed deserted, and there wasn't much traffic on this seldom traveled route. I glanced at the sky; the rain stopped as quickly as it had begun, and dirty clouds streaked across the moon. I halfway expected to see an old hag sailing past on a broom, and wished I had brought someone—anyone—for company.

Cotton plants marched in knee-high rows in the field

across from the woods, and I pulled into a rutted dirt
lane where ragged weeds screened my car from view.
Snatching my raincoat and a flashlight, I crossed the
dreary stretch of road and stood at the edge of the woods.
Something was happening here tonight. But where? And
when? It had been after eleven when I left home; it must
be nearly midnight. The witching hour. I pulled the raincoat about me, protecting my head with the hood. My
fingers gripped the flashlight until they ached, but I didn't
turn it on. Although I couldn't see anyone, I knew I
wasn't alone.

I sensed them before I heard them, the somber group
passing through the trees like a drab procession of
monks. I pressed close to a pine and felt the sticky resin
come off on my hands as the silent column crept past.
Eleven dark figures, hoods concealing their faces, walked
with bowed heads. Some carried candles, flickering in the
moist air; others held what looked like a long staff. The
person who brought up the rear, I noticed, lugged a bulging sack the size of a pillowcase, and whatever was in the
sack squirmed. My stomach squirmed, too.

I watched them disappear over a small rise, and it was
as though they had never been there. Not even a candle's
glow betrayed their presence. Was I imagining things? I
sniffed. I could smell the hot tallow. What I had seen was
real, but what was I supposed to do? I held to the tree for
support. What was I doing in this ghastly place?

I remembered what Fred O'Leary had said about the
last sinister meeting in the woods. "They slipped out on
us," he told me. "Vanished like they weren't ever there."
But where had they gone? I stepped from behind my tree
and circled the cedar-rimmed hummock. At least I could
try to follow.

The moon gave just enough light through the trees to
enable me to see if I walked slowly and carefully. The
flashlight, of course, was useless. It would give me away
immediately. I was glad of my raincoat, even though the
night was warm. Its dark color made me less conspicuous
and hid my face—made me almost like one of them.

Ahead I heard them chanting in some tongue I didn't understand, and the sound of it repelled me. The cadence seemed vaguely familiar—but wrong. Tiny lights circled and wavered; cloaks billowed in the eerie glow.

I crouched in the underbrush watching, disgusted at the chill of anticipation I felt. The mystery of the bizarre ritual challenged my curiosity. I wanted to draw closer. . . .

The moaning grew louder as the leader lifted his long, curved blade and led his (or her?) followers in a writhing dance among the circle of stones. I crept deeper into my cover, gripping my raincoat about me, but I couldn't seem to get warm; the cold went right through me. I watched as one of the number brought a small animal from the bag. It wiggled and whimpered in its efforts to escape. I clamped a hand over my mouth, feeling the bile rise inside me. It was a puppy!

With the sword, the tall leader sketched a symbol in the earth as candles were placed in a circle. The terrified dog was held on the stone altar as worshippers swayed, undulating, repeating their singsong incantation. I felt as if I had turned to marble. They were going to kill that puppy and use its blood in their grisly rite. From a distance I heard the throbbing of a motor. It seemed to be drawing closer. Reaching out in the darkness, my hand closed over a stick. If I could distract them for a second, maybe the dog would have a chance.

The group scattered as the stick landed in the circle, and to my relief, the puppy scampered into the woods. I grabbed my chest with both hands to hold my heart inside. Now what? Could I outrace them to my car. I braced myself to run. Maybe they wouldn't see me.

"Where'd that stick come from?" a man's voice said. "One of you catch that damned dog!"

"Somebody's out there!" said another.

I squinted as a flashlight shone about, bobbing in the blackness around me; I knelt, motionless, as the bright beam passed me by.

"Aw, it's just the wind—forget it!"

I stiffened at the sound of the voice. I looked at the man who had spoken. The hood had slipped from his face just enough to expose the dark hair, the clean cut of his chin: Jericho Scott.

Dry leaves rustled at my feet, and something soft and wet nuzzled my ankles. I gasped as the puppy clamored about me, yelping his introductions, announcing my presence to the dark-shrouded cult.

Chapter Fifteen

"**T**here he is! Get him!"

"I told you somebody was there. Don't let him get away." Red flames flared from the pit; dark figures stirred, their harsh voices clamoring. Soon I would be surrounded. I snatched the puppy and ran into blackness, hoping the night and the trees would envelope me, protect me until I could reach the car.

But the Widow's Woods weren't friendly. If this place had a soul—and I was certain it did—it was as black as the ever-present shadows. Briars tore at my clothing; roots and stones seemed to sprout in my path, causing me to stumble. I half slid, half ran down a slate-slick incline, skidding in the gravel at the bottom, and hesitated briefly before plunging into the dense undergrowth to my left. I knew they were behind me, possibly all around me, but they didn't make any noise.

The puppy wiggled to get down and yelped when I hoisted it roughly to my shoulder. The sharp metal tag that dangled from its collar bit into my neck. Behind me I heard the scuffle of feet on the forest floor, and the bright beams of a flashlight searched me out once more. I closed my eyes against the glare, clutched the puppy against my chest, and took a running dive into what appeared to be a shallow drop-off. It wasn't.

125

I heard them murmuring above me, saw their pale swords of light crisscrossing the night. I knelt in a nest of honeysuckle and felt the dog's soft fur beneath my chin; its heartbeat blended with my own. I seemed to have rolled into some kind of wide, tunnel-like ditch, and my knee had struck a rock on the way down. A sharp pain ran through it when I tried to stand. Somewhere not very far away—to my right, I thought—a vehicle moved down the lonely stretch of road. If I could just make it to my car, maybe I would have a chance.

"I hear him! There he is—down there. Hurry, we've got him now." It was a rough, young voice—a woman's voice. I took a deep breath and plunged ahead, shoving my way past pine seedlings and underbrush. The sharp, fresh scent of evergreens briefly overcame the heavier smell of humus. The puppy whimpered. It didn't matter now. Nothing mattered but reaching the road and safety. I heard the rustle of leaves behind me, the pounding of footsteps on the uneven ground. It was too late for caution.

Hands brushed the folds of my raincoat, and someone grabbed my arm; I jerked away. There were two of them upon me—maybe three—and I had run down like a windup toy. It hurt to breathe. I didn't know who these idiots were, but I knew I hated them and would kick and claw till the very end. I gathered all my strength, turned, and body-rammed my closest attacker. The contact made me dizzy.

He fell with an oath and a thump that shook the earth beneath us, but the other one was still behind me. Through the thinning trees I saw the shine of wet asphalt as a wan moon peeked from clearing skies. I was almost there, and my pursuer seemed to be slowing, dropping behind. Then I saw why. A truck was coming.

I burst into the clearing as it lumbered past, spraying the roadsides with muddy water, and splashed across its wake, not daring to look over my shoulder. My car waited like a familiar friend behind its cover of Queen Anne's lace and blackberry bushes. The air felt lighter here, purer. I scrambled behind the wheel and turned the key in the switch. Everything was going to be all right.

Nothing happened. I pumped the gas pedal and frantically turned the key again. Something was wrong. There was no connection. I might as well be trying to start that rusting old tractor in the shed behind the field. Across the road a dark figure moved from tree to tree. Another walked at a crouch beside a fence waiting for a chance to follow, and others wouldn't be far behind. I refused to wait here for them—trapped like a bird in a cage.

I slipped out to the ground and crawled through the tall grass to the old shed. The puppy squirmed in my arms and licked my face with its wet tongue. "Don't try to make up to me, you Benedict Arnold!" I whispered, pressing close to the wall. "If it hadn't been for you, I might not be in this mess." But the dog was not the reason I came to the woods tonight, unless it knew how to write! Could it have been Jericho Scott who left the note about Papa Sam at my door? How could I have let myself be so trusting? Would I never learn? But I had hoped—wanted —needed to believe in someone again.

I allowed myself a minute to catch my breath. I couldn't see a thing from where I hid. I might be surrounded by now. Somehow I had to get back to the road! A plane droned overhead, its lights winking in the sky. How I wished I were on it! Not far away to my left overhanging bushes outlined a creek which eventually crossed under the road. Taking advantage of the noise of the plane, I quickly rolled beneath the barbed wire fence, shoving the dog ahead of me, and ran for the dubious protection of the creek. Dark cattle stood zombielike and stared at me. Black Angus, probably. I hoped none of them was a bull! I gasped aloud as my sneakered foot sank into something soft and oozy. I knew it wasn't mud.

"In the pasture! See him? Over there—he has the dog!"

I heard them shouting among themselves on the other side of the fence, heard the soft scraping of their feet on the dirt road beside the cotton field. They were only a few

127

yards behind me. I didn't even take time to look over my shoulder. I was tired. So tired.

At first I thought it was the plane again, the soft, distant vibrating of a motor; but as it drew nearer and louder, I realized that someone on a motorcycle had buzzed up the narrow, rutted road. Reinforcements, no doubt. I shoved my way through a tangle of brambles on the creek bank. When I looked back, my pursuers had scattered, and the man on the motorcycle circled the field, the beam from his headlights painting a yellow stripe in the night. I sat on a rock with the dog in my lap and cried. When I looked up the cyclist was gone. Was he the leader of the pack rounding up his motley band for a fresh attack, or was he dispersing them for another reason? I didn't know, didn't care, but the interruption gave me the time I needed and I took advantage of it.

I let the foliage screen me from view as I made my way to the road, and hesitated in the darkness under the narrow wooden bridge when a car rumbled overhead. How was I to know if it was one of *them?* Yet somehow I had to get back to town, and the burning pain in my knee was getting worse. Carefully I rolled up my pants and bathed the sticky blood away with creek water. It was cool, and soothed the pain for a little while at least.

It would have been difficult enough walking in the lumpy fields beside the road in daylight, but the darkness made it even more troublesome, the long grass switched my legs, and every chigger in the county feasted on my ankles. I stopped to scratch a bite on my shin, then froze as headlights approached from the direction I had come. Grabbing the puppy to me, I squatted in the weeds as the car passed. I was glad I did. Jericho Scott drove slowly, as if he were looking for something—or someone. I waited until his taillights disappeared from sight before I vaulted over the ditch and crossed to the other side. If he planned to turn around and come back, I wanted more distance between us.

How far was I from home? The woods always seemed so close—almost in my backyard. It couldn't be much farther. Under other circumstances I might have enjoyed the walk. The dusky countryside was skimmed in white, the trees streaked with silver. Frogs carried on their raspy conversations in the grass, and owls called in the woods beside the road. I hugged the sleeping little dog like a muff and buried my fear and pain inside me. My body— at least for the time being—felt numb, but my spirit was almost serene. Hadn't I outwitted them? Wasn't I almost home?

I stiffened as a car pulled to a sudden stop beside me. A light shone in my face!

"Are you all right, miss? Is anything wrong?" It was a man's voice. I couldn't see his face.

I closed my eyes against the glare and staggered backward as my foot sank into a post hole.

"Give me a hand here, Leland, she needs help!" A woman spoke; firm hands reached out to me, pulled me to my feet. The woman was young, black, capable, measuring the situation with alert brown eyes. She must be new in town; I didn't know her. The man was white, probably in his sixties, with a hint of a potbelly and coffee on his breath. I had seen him before. They both wore the blue summer uniform of the city police. Two people had called to report the activity in the woods, said it looked like trouble in the making, they told me.

"I don't give a hang if these fruitcakes worship grandma's drawers," the man said. "But those woods are private property, and they're trespassing." He scanned the empty road in both directions as if he hoped a dark-robed figure would materialize. "They've got no business messing around out there with fire. Just about burned the blasted place down once this summer."

I thought that might be for the best, but I kept my opinion to myself. I showed them the puppy who was busily trying to chew a button off my raincoat.

"Why, that's the Swenson's dog!" The woman examined the tag. "They've been looking for it all day. They live clear on the other side of town. How'd it get way over here?"

I told her what I had seen in the woods and what I was doing there. "They followed me across the road, but my car wouldn't start," I said. "I think somebody tampered with it." I hesitated, removing my shoes before getting into the patrol car. "I've run through the pasture," I explained in an aside to the woman, whose name I learned was Sergeant Totherow, "crawled around in the woods, and slid down the creek bank. I'll have to soak for a week to get clean."

The policewoman smiled. "It's okay. We've hauled worse." She waited while her partner radioed headquarters. "I know you're eager to get that bath, but we'd like for you to show us where all this happened. These cultists, or whoever they are, are probably all gone by now, but we just might get lucky." She spoke as if she hoped they would. I hoped they wouldn't, but I agreed to go along. A backup car was to meet us there in case anything was going on.

But the Widow's Woods were dark and silent, a formidable fortress of trees; not even a rabbit scurried in the murky undergrowth. "Who does this place belong to?" the policewoman asked.

"Why, the Kennemores," Leland said. "Always has. All this land around here used to belong to them, you know. This is about all that's left." He turned and looked at me. "You know that Dillard Moore? The one they arrested the other day? Well, it's his aunt owns it—that kinda funny little lady—used to teach over at the high school."

"Miss Baby?"

"Yeah, that's the one. From what I hear, this is about all she's got, and if they don't quit playing around with fire out here, she won't even have it."

Well, at least Miss Baby had inherited something, I thought, although if the woods were my inheritance, I think I'd just as soon be left out altogether.

When the second police car came I told them how to find the area where the ritual took place, while Leland looked at my car. "I don't see anything wrong under the hood," he said, thrusting about with a flashlight. "Keys inside?"

I nodded. "I left them in the ignition . . . but it isn't going to start. They did something to—"

I felt as if someone had knocked the breath out of me as the motor turned over with its familiar drone.

Leland lifted an eyebrow. "Sounds fine to me. You must've been in too much of a hurry. Probably flooded the engine."

"But it wasn't like that." I turned to the woman for reassurance. "Something was wrong with it—really! It wouldn't crank at all."

I felt the sergeant's eyes measuring me in the dark. "Did you say somebody left you a note? Why would they do that?"

I shook my head. "I don't know, unless they knew I was worried about my grandfather." I shrugged. "I guess I'd do just about anything if I thought he was really in trouble."

"Do you have it now?" she asked.

I yawned. "Have what?"

"The note. The one you say was left at your door."

I felt in my pockets and remembered. "I left it in my shorts," I said.

"Well, in any case, you're in no shape to drive," she said. "We'll get one of the others to bring your car in for you."

I leaned back against the seat in the musty police car and closed my eyes. Let them believe what they would, someone had tampered with my car; but just then I didn't have the energy to argue. The puppy had gotten wet in the creek and smelled worse than I did, and my knee hurt like the devil. If I weren't so tired and miserable, I could go to sleep right here.

The sputtering radio woke me. "They've cleared out," the voice reported, "but they were up to their usual devilment all right. Ashes still hot, and candles about burned to the ground."

"Any tire tracks? Signs of vehicles?" Leland asked.

"Nothing! Course it's too dark to see your hand in front of you; all we found was a burlap sack. I'll swear, I don't know where these loonies come from!"

"Or where in the hell they go," Leland muttered to his partner. "Oh well, maybe something will turn up tomorrow in the daylight, but I doubt it. It's downright spooky the way these creeps disappear."

Sergeant Totherow sat in the back with me as we drove into town. "You say these people wore hoods. I don't suppose you recognized any of them?"

I shifted the puppy to the floor and found he had wet on my leg. "You wouldn't have a towel, would you?"

The woman passed me a box of tissues. "You heard a couple of them speak, you said. Were any of their voices familiar?"

I blotted my lap with a wad of tissue. "No . . . I don't think so. . . . I'm not sure."

"Sleep on it," the sergeant said. "Maybe something will come to you." She turned away, but I could tell I was still in her range of vision. "I suppose it's occurred to you that somebody lured you out there to get you away from the house?"

It hadn't, but I waited on the screen porch while the officers checked my house. Cooter had neatly folded the afghan I'd given him and left it at one end of the glider before abandoning me for home and bed, and a low light still burned in the bedroom of Jericho Scott's apartment. In the darkness it was impossible to see if his car was parked in its customary spot. Why had I lied about seeing Jericho in the woods? If that hadn't been him at the macabre ceremony, it must have been his twin. And why had he wanted me to think he was spending the evening at home?

After the police left I wearily dragged myself upstairs and let the shower pummel me clean. It was after two in the morning, and Sudie's bed was empty. I winced as I bandaged my lacerated knee. I missed the puppy already; I could have used his company. Again I checked the lock on the door to my room before turning off the light, pausing once more at the window. Next door Eulonia's house was quiet, but across the yard at Jericho's a shadow moved by the window. I yawned in spite of myself. I was too tired even to hate. Tomorrow I would find out the reason for this man's peculiar behavior.

I groped my way to bed, listening for the sound of Sudie's key in the door and wishing for once that my friend hadn't become such a night owl. The two police officers had found no signs of any intruder, and everything seemed to be in its usual place, yet I had an uneasy feeling somebody had been in the house while I was gone.

Chapter Sixteen

The shrilling of the telephone, insistent as a siren, brought me abruptly awake. I rubbed my eyes and stretched, regretting it as pain stabbed my injured knee. But I was alive, the sun was shining, and I was here, relatively safe, in my own bed. My whole body ached as I rolled over and reached for the phone.

"Well, I wasn't sure if I would find you there or not!" Sudie's voice was caustic, like vinegar in an open wound.

"What?" I propped myself on an elbow. "Sudie?" I glanced at the bed beside mine. It hadn't been slept in. "Where are you? Look, it's none of my business if you want to stay out all night, but at least you could've let me know!"

"But—you—Let *you* know! What are you talking about?"

I took a deep breath and paused. "You're the one who didn't come home!" I stuffed a pillow beneath my head and shifted to the cooler side of the bed, shouting when I straightened my sore knee.

"Maybe I'd better call at a more convenient time." Sudie's voice could have frozen bootleg whiskey.

"Will you please come to the point and tell me what's wrong?" I said. "I'm not in much of a mood for guessing games."

"You know very well what I mean: Jericho Scott. He's there, isn't he?"

"I haven't seen Jericho Scott since yesterday," I admitted. His name on my lips sounded hollow, sad.

"Uh-oh!" Sudie was silent for a minute. "Then where were you last night? Who put that note on your door?"

"What note? When?"

"Not long after twelve, I guess. Nelson and I went to a concert in Spartanburg, and there was a note on your door when we got back." She sighed. "Jane, it *looked* like your handwriting."

"What'd it say?"

"That you were going out with Jericho and didn't know when or if you'd be home, so I was not to worry about spending the night. Sounds like somebody wanted me out of the way. Jane, where were you? What's going on?"

I told her. I told her of finding the note luring me to the Widow's Woods, and of being chased by a bunch of crazies wearing cowls. I even told about the appearance of the stranger on the motorcycle and of my rescue by local police. But I didn't tell her about seeing Jericho Scott.

"That man on the motorcycle! Was he the same one you saw in Eulonia's kitchen?"

"I don't know. It was dark, and he was too far away. Besides, all motorcycles sound alike to me."

Whoever had sent me on that wild excursion in the woods certainly hadn't had my best interests at heart. I had recognized Jericho's voice, but the others were only a jumble. I ate my cereal on the back steps to avoid being in the house alone. The gash on my knee looked red and puffy and I walked like Frankenstein's monster. I knew I should let a doctor treat it, but first I had another, more important errand.

The carriage house next door was silent, and the red Mustang was gone. Its owner was probably out getting his tongue oiled. And since he didn't seem to make a habit of locking his door, this would be a good time to do a little spying. If Jericho Scott came home and found me snooping—fine. I hoped he would. I almost smiled as I hobbled up the steep wooden steps to his second floor quarters. Who was it who said that about bearding the lion in his den? I was sure Jericho would know.

A lone spider spun her web in the overhang, and paint peeled from the once-white railings. I hesitated at the door where sunlight sliced through the blinds and lay in pale slats on the braided living room rug. Otherwise, the room was in darkness. I stepped inside and let my eyes become accustomed to it. Heavy draperies of a red and blue paisley pattern covered the two front windows, and I jerked them aside to let in the sun. The air conditioner was not running, and the apartment was stifling. It was also oddly austere.

I looked about me. The typewriter was missing from the desk, and the stereo no longer sat on the shelf beside it. Except for a few dishes drying in the rack by the sink, the kitchen countertops were uncluttered. I hurried to the bedroom, knowing what I would find. Jericho's books were gone, and the covers had been stripped from the bed. The place was desolate, sterile, as if no one had ever lived there.

I ran outside as fast as my knee would allow and clung to the narrow railing, absorbing what had become obvious. My handsome, well-read neighbor had left sometime during the night—and he didn't intend to come back. One more strike and I'm out, I thought. But I didn't plan to play anymore.

"If you're lookin' for that writer guy, he took off early this morning. Never did get around to fixin' that back step!" Dillard Moore sat in the wisteria arbor eating a bunch of grapes. He stared at each one before he put it into his mouth, as if it held the key to some deep mystery. "Who are you?" he said.

I told him. His eyes looked funny—scary funny, and I started slowly down the steps. The massive hulk of Twin Towers was only a few yards away, but Miss Baby might never hear me . . . and what could she do if she did?

"I remember you from the police station," Dillard went on. "They think I broke into that house; I didn't. Hell, I

had my own key, but I didn't use it that night." He considered another grape.

I put a few more feet between us and glanced at the
arched window in the tower. Rapunzel should be there,
letting down her hair. But she wasn't; nobody was
around but Dillard Moore and me. Should I dare? "Where
did you get a key?" I asked.

He laughed, slowly twirling the cluster of grapes. "Had
one made from that key she kept under the pot."

"Why?"

"Let's just say I liked her taste in booze. My aunt
doesn't drink, you know: 'Lips that touch liquor . . . '
and all that! Gets kinda dry around here." He slouched in
his seat and looked up at me with vacant eyes in a pasty
face. "I'll bet you drink, though, don't you?"

I thought about Etta Lucas carrying his baby and it
made me sick. And Chloe. Had he really been out of town
when Chloe was killed? Maybe she had discovered him
raiding her liquor cabinet. And there was something else
that repulsed me—something in the slope of his shoulders and that nasty little undercurrent of depravity in his
voice. I was almost sure he had been with that group in
the woods the night before!

"You're one of them, aren't you? One of those so-called
Satan worshippers who go around robbing graves and
killing animals. Couldn't you just join the Rotary or
Kiwanis like everybody else? It's sick! Why do you do it?"

Why had I said that? Had I lost my mind completely? I
might as well offer myself for sacrifice.

From the dark look on his face I thought he was going
to come after me, but the effort was too much for him. He
squeezed the grape from its skin and rolled it around in
his mouth, casting the peeling aside. "Why? Can't tell you
that; it's a secret." Dillard Moore laughed again. "Lots of
secrets in the Widow's Woods."

I nodded mutely. If I stood still enough long enough,
maybe he would forget I was there; and I was right. Soon
he closed his eyes and nodded, slumped forward on the
bench. I turned and walked slowly, quietly across the

grass, through the still orchard, and home. I bolted every door.

Should I tell the police what Dillard Moore had said about having a key to Chloe's side of the house? From the kitchen window I saw the Baptist minister getting into his car after visiting Eulonia Moody. Jericho had warned me not to tell about my neighbor and the man on the motorcycle—but then Jericho was a classics-quoting snake in the grass. I wondered if he had given my identity away to the others last night in the woods. Even if he wasn't the one who left the note, he must have recognized my car. Did the cultists know who I was? Where I lived?

Sudie asked the same question when she came over later. "Did any of them see your face? Could you see theirs?"

"I don't think so," I said. "They mistook me for a man under my raincoat, and I wasn't going to tell them different!" I told her what Dillard Moore had said and that he had as good as admitted taking part in the rituals in the woods. "Of course he was so stoned, he'd admit to being a Martian, so it probably doesn't mean a thing.

"I don't know why Miss Baby stays on in that place! It's big and ugly, and she can't keep it up. I'd get a nice little house somewhere and unload Dillard once and for all!"

Sudie shrugged. "Well, it's home I guess. She doesn't have much else."

"She has the woods," I told her. "Did you know that tract was left to her?"

She nodded. "And if Dillard and his weird buddies don't burn it down, she could come into some money. A developer was looking at it a few months ago; the last I heard, he was still interested. Wants to put one of those exclusive residential areas there—golf course, country club, and everything. If the deal goes through, Miss Baby could buy her own Roman villa."

"And if anything happens to Miss Baby, Dillard Moore could buy his own drugstore," I said.

Later, after Sudie insisted on chauffeuring me to the doctor, I was ensconced in the back porch hammock with a pitcher of lemonade and six stitches in my knee when the telephone rang. "Miss Baby," Sudie mouthed, handing me the receiver.

"Jane? I'm glad I caught you at home, dear." She spoke in a subdued voice and I wondered if Dillard was lurking about somewhere. "You had asked me about the students' involvement in the occult, and I heard something which might be of interest, I think . . ."

"Yes, ma'am?" I looked at Sudie and shrugged.

"As you may remember, I tutor sometimes during the summer months, and one of my students inadvertently let slip a remark I found most curious." She paused, and I could picture her standing there tucking in strands of hair as she often did in class. "I believe some of the young people plan something like a séance tonight in that abandoned church out on Miller's Pond Road. They say they're going to try to bring back the spirit of Etta Lucas."

I wondered if her spaced-out nephew had anything to do with this and if Miss Baby were aware of his involvement in what went on in the woods. I sank back into the hammock and closed my eyes. "Which church is that, Miss Baby?"

"It's that little yellow stone building not far from town —sits back in a pine grove. Used to be East End Baptist, but they moved when the congregation grew."

"And you're sure it's tonight?"

"From what I was able to glean; of course that's always subject to change. You know how these teenagers are."

I almost laughed. My former teacher spoke as if we were contemporaries.

"I wouldn't go out there at night alone," the woman continued. "It just wouldn't be a wise thing to do."

I agreed that it wouldn't. In fact, I had no intention of going to the old church at night at all. But I saw no harm in checking it out in the daylight—as soon as Sudie left to give her piano lesson.

She did everything but wring her hands as she prepared to leave. "I don't like leaving you here by yourself like this, especially with that maniac over there," she

140

said, opening and shutting the screen door for the third time. "If it weren't that little Mabry girl who's already missed two lessons, I'd stay here with you. Now be sure and latch this after I've gone."

"I will, don't worry; I'll ask Shagg to come over. Besides, I'm sure Cooter's around somewhere."

"Haven't you heard? Leola slipped in the bathroom this morning and broke her ankle. She probably has poor Cooter chained to the kitchen stove!" She paused with a hand on the door. "Have you heard anything from Papa Sam?"

"Not a word, and I'm really getting worried now. I've called and called, but nobody answers. Where do you suppose he went?"

Sudie frowned. "I wish I knew. It has to have something to do with all that's been going on. Your grandpa isn't one to just sit around doing nothing."

I had to agree. Papa Sam liked to fight his own battles. I only hoped he hadn't gotten in over his head.

After Sudie left I called Shagg as I promised her I would, but no one answered; I remembered he was still on his shift at the recreation center, so I left a message telling him where I would be. What Sudie lacked in a spirit of adventure, Shagg more than made up for, and I had hoped he would be able to go with me to the old church. After all, these kids were his students, and he did seem to care about them. Maybe he could influence them as well. Besides, I really didn't like going there alone.

I allowed Sudie a few minutes to get to her lesson before driving in the opposite direction toward Miller's Pond Road and the old East End Baptist Church. I hoped the local anesthetic the doctor had given me would last until I got home.

The cotton mill that had once thrived on the east end of Sweetsprings had long since been torn down, but the small frame houses of its workers remained. Now owned by individuals, each cottage seemed to strive to be different from its neighbors: some in the color of paint, others by the addition of rooms or trim. The East End Baptist

Church was almost hidden in a thicket of pines several blocks past the old mill site and at least a quarter of a mile from the nearest house. I turned into a narrow gravel road edged with wild plum and dogwood and drove slowly into the dim closeness of the pine woods. At first glance the little church seemed to be cared for, and then I saw the broken windows, crumbling cement steps, and wisteria growing rampant along the yellow stone walls. The now-familiar five-pointed star and an upside down cross had been spray-painted on the door, and the numbers 666 were scratched on the fading paint above it.

I don't know how long I sat in the car staring, not wanting to believe what I saw. I had heard of things like this happening; now I had to accept the truth. Even though the building was no longer used as a place of worship, it had once been a Christian church—and now it was defiled, desecrated. It was sickening—and sad, too that these kids had nothing better to do.

I sat for a minute listening for the sound of Shagg's car. It was after five o'clock—time for his shift at the center to be over, but he didn't always go home after work, which meant he might not get my message until much later. Shakily I limped from the car and sank onto the bottom step where the building gave welcome shade, leaned against the rough banister, and closed my eyes; I would give him a few more minutes.

But the pricking in my knee made me aware that feeling would soon return, and I lurched to my feet and waded through drifts of leaves to the entrance of the church. The double oak doors were warped so they didn't close properly, but I tugged at one until I was able to slip inside. The building smelled of filth and decay, but light came from high windows on each side and from a platter-size hole in the roof just above the choir loft. Rain had left remains of rot and debris on the hardwood floor, and the ceiling above the altar was stained with smoke. The dead, gray scent was stifling.

I wandered down what had once been the center aisle. The pews were gone, but I could see outlines of where

142

they once stood. Vandals had scrawled swastikas on the dirt-streaked walls, and painted a huge circled A, the symbol of anarchy, on the side of the baptistry. Charred ashes from a wood fire remained in a rusty wheelbarrow at the front of the room in the center of a crude pentagram.

Somewhere in the back of the church a board creaked and I looked around for a place to hide, then jumped at the sound of tires on the gravel drive outside. A car door slammed; then another. Shagg must have brought someone with him.

"Hey, look! Somebody's inside! Whose car is that?" A girl spoke. I didn't recognize her voice.

"Beats me! Maybe Rodney's got new wheels." This time the speaker was familiar: Nathan Lovejoy.

"Maybe we'd better not go in . . . somebody might . . ."

"Oh, don't be stupid, Kristabelle. Rodney and Vance said they'd be here, didn't they? Besides, nobody cares about this old church anymore. Come on."

Dragging my stiff leg, I stepped around a stack of firewood, kicked aside empty beer cans, and hurried into a tiny room beneath the choir loft. The one small window had been painted over, but there was enough light to distinguish the limp, still form on the floor. I stooped over to see the stubble of beard, hair matted with blood. His wrist was cold to the touch.

Dillard Moore would not be scaring me—or anyone else—again.

Chapter Seventeen

I'm not going to scream, I decided, stumbling backward into a rickety table and knocking a bottle to the floor. It landed with a harsh *clunk* and banged against the wall. When I turned to steady myself, my fingers came within an inch of touching the bloody hammer that must have been used to kill Dillard Moore. Then I screamed.

"Who's back there?" Nathan called. "Cut the crap now, Rodney. Is that you?"

The two of them were stacking supplies beside their makeshift altar when I stepped into the sanctuary, and when they saw me, it was a race to see who could reach the outside first.

"Hey, wait a minute, Nathan! It's me—Jane Cannon!" I stood on the bottom step of the platform and watched them. I wasn't going to chase them; I couldn't catch them, anyway. "It isn't going to do any good to run. We've got a problem here—a bad one." I drew in my breath. God, I wished Shagg were here! I wasn't doing a very good job of this.

But Nathan whirled about at the door and Kristabelle stepped up beside him. The boy glared at me. "What kind of problem?"

"You know a guy named Dillard Moore?"

The two exchanged glances. They knew him. Nathan shrugged; Kristabelle stared at the floor. "Yeah, I guess," she said.

"Well, he's in that little room back there," I told them. "And he's dead. Looks like somebody bashed in his head." I knew I was being callous, but three people had been murdered, and I wasn't feeling so great myself.

Neither was Kristabelle. Her face turned pale and she covered her mouth with both hands and ran outside. I followed, shoving Nathan in front of me. I had had enough of darkness and death.

"We'll have to call the police," I told them as we sat shivering in the sunlight. "It looks like whoever killed him left the weapon behind. Maybe they can get some prints." Kristabelle Douglas had cried her way through half a box of tissues, and I wished I could join her. Except for the returning pain in my knee, I felt numb—oddly removed from what was happening around me.

"They'll want to know what we were doing here." The girl sniffed. "Nathan and I haven't seen him—Dillard— since Shelba Jean disappeared. We didn't even know he was in there!"

Nathan had gone back inside to retrieve the collection he'd left by the altar, and had hurriedly tossed the objects into the back of his car. I made a point to see them, although he tried to block my view.

"Where'd you get that book?" I demanded, pointing to a rusty black volume buried beneath a world history text.

"What book?" Nathan winced as he accidentally bumped his leg while trying to close the car door.

"This thing here. . . . Good lord, Nathan! Surely you don't believe this stuff!" I plucked it from the pile and studied the title. *"The Treasury of Witchcraft* . . . I guess this is research for a term paper! And I see you've brought your Ouija board, too. Is that how you plan to get in touch with Etta?" I tossed the book aside. "What have you done to your leg?"

"I told him he oughta see a doctor," Kristabelle said as Nathan limped to the steps.

"Shut up, Kristabelle!" The boy slumped beside her, obviously making an effort not to cry out. "How'd you know that about Etta? That we were going to try to reach her tonight?"

"Never mind that." I stood over him, casting a long shadow across the steps. "Let me see your leg, Nathan!" I tried not to gasp when I saw the infected wound across the upper part of his calf. "That's a bad cut. How did it happen? Why haven't you done something about it?"

Silently Nathan rolled down the leg of his pants. I could tell he was debating whether or not to tell me.

"That gash looks deep; it needs stitches, Nathan." I looked at Kristabelle, but the girl only sighed and put her head in her hands. No help there. "Okay, get gangrene and hobble around on one leg for the rest of your life!" I shook my head. "It's not going to get any better . . . and when those little red streaks start—"

"I've been cleaning it with antiseptic! I change the bandage twice a day!" Nathan frantically rolled up his pants leg again. "I don't see any red streaks."

"How did you get that cut?" I asked.

Kristabelle Douglas raised her head. "He did it himself," she said, "with your granddaddy's sword!"

Nathan had taken the sword, I learned, as a part of his initiation rite into something called "The Sorcerer's Circle," an elite group within a cult composed mostly of teens. "I was supposed to kill this kitten," he said, "and smear its blood on my face." The boy stared ahead of him as he spoke. His eyes had a curious, blank expression. "They left me alone in the woods to do it . . . but I couldn't. . . ."

Kristabelle looked at Nathan and smiled. "He turned the kitten loose and cut himself on the leg—told them it ran off into the bushes to die."

"Looks like you did a thorough job of it," I said.

"There had to be a lot of blood on the ground to look convincing," Nathan told me. "And I bound my leg with a handkerchief so it wouldn't give me away—still it came through, but I blamed it on the cat."

The thought of it made me sick. "But why?" I asked. "This was obviously something you found appalling. Why did you want to join?"

Kristabelle and Nathan looked at one another. The girl spoke first. "We might as well tell her. Everybody's gonna find out anyhow."

At first the group seemed mysterious, exciting, Nathan explained, and they were selective in their membership. It was an honor to be asked to join. "Nobody had to do stupid things then," he added, "like killing animals and stuff. We played Dungeons and Dragons some, messed around with séances, smoked a little pot, drank some beer—things like that."

I nodded, trying to maintain a stoical expression; Ruby Lovejoy would wet her bloomers if she knew what her grandson had been doing. "What happened?" I asked.

"It was that Dillard Moore!" Nathan clasped his thin hands together. "He got it on with some of the girls—wanted to make a regular orgy of it—a real degenerate slimeball. But Shelba Jean was the one he really liked."

"And did Shelba Jean go along with this?" I asked.

Kristabelle shrugged. "For a while, but then she got tired of him. She always does. I think she met somebody new at the beach." She twisted the collar of her shirt. "Dillard didn't like being dumped. He used to have a thing for Etta Lucas, you know, but she told him to get lost. . . . I think he killed her—maybe both of them!" She leaned against Nathan's shoulder and he put a skinny arm around her. "See, Dillard was mean like that," she said. "Spiteful. He threatened to tell things on all of us—things we wouldn't want people to know."

"Like what?" I knew I was being merciless, but recess was over.

Kristabelle looked up at me as she moved away from Nathan. "Just things—you know—things we were doing."

I didn't know, but I could guess. Kristabelle was taller than most boys her age, she had absolutely no shape, and her front teeth protruded a little. Nathan Lovejoy was a good student but a poor athlete and had always been kind

of a loner. The two of them were probably eager to belong, to feel accepted, and they had gone along with
whatever was expected of them until it was too late to
turn around. I looked at the pair of them on the steps.
They were sixteen, maybe seventeen years old, but looked
younger. They also looked scared. Fear had whittled
away at their confidence, their self-esteem, and left them
like defensive little animals. I knew something about
that.

"So he was blackmailing you?" And no telling how
many others, I thought. No wonder somebody smashed
in Dillard Moore's treacherous head. "Tell me about Etta.
Was she involved in all this black magic stuff? Did you
know her well?"

"Yeah, sort of. We used to run around together some
last year, but she didn't have much to do with us after
Christmas."

Kristabelle snickered. "Got too big for her britches—in
more ways than one."

Nathan Lovejoy groaned. "Oh, shit! Can't you keep your
mouth shut, Kristabelle?"

I leaned against the rough stone banister. "Never mind.
I know—she was pregnant. Was it Dillard's?"

"Why do you think her parents sent her to Columbia?
To get her away from Dillard Moore and that bunch—
only it was too late." Kristabelle plucked a dandelion
from a crack in the walk and blew away the fuzz.

"I think she knew," Nathan said quietly. "I think she
knew she was going to die."

"What do you mean?" I felt cold again.

"I don't know. It was just the way she acted—like she
was scared to death and didn't know what to do about it,"
he said. "She hadn't told anybody about the baby yet—not
even her parents. They didn't find out until afterwards. . . ."

I frowned. Sudie had told me that Etta's mother was
under a doctor's care, and her parents had sold their
house and left Sweetsprings to avoid the reminder.

"Are you sure Dillard Moore was the father?" I asked.

Nathan smiled for the first time since I'd seen him. "Well, it sure as hell wasn't me!"

I stood when I heard the distant sounds of a motor. "Is that your friends, Rodney and Vance?"

Nathan frowned. "How'd you know about them?"

"I heard you say they were meeting you here."

"Huh! Those two are long gone! If they saw you out here with us, you think they'd stick around?" Nathan stood slowly, favoring his injured leg.

"Some loyal friends you have," I told him. "What were you going to do in there anyway—besides drink beer, I mean?"

"Vance said he could bring Etta back," Nathan told me. "He was gonna borrow this crystal ball—a real one, he said—from a medium he knows, and we were gonna try and find out who killed her. 'Course if it was Dillard, it doesn't really matter now, does it?" He stood listening quietly. "That couldn't be Rodney and Vance anyway. It's a motorcycle, and it's not getting closer, it's going away."

I looked at my watch. Sudie would be back by now and wondering where I was. "I think we'd better go on and get the police," I said.

We had reached the end of the long, pine-lined drive when Shagg Henry screeched to a stop in front of us, and in spite of my injured knee, I jumped from my car and ran to him, throwing both arms around his neck. "Am I glad to see you! Somebody's bashed in Dillard Moore's head and left him inside the church!"

"Whoa! Hold on a minute!" Shagg's large hand encircled my wrist as he noticed the young couple in the other car. "What are you two doing here?"

Nathan and Kristabelle had a decidedly squirmy look, as if they would rather be anywhere else. I didn't blame them. "Could we save that for later," I said, "and get back to Dillard? There's no telling how long he's been lying there."

"Doesn't sound like he's going anywhere," Shagg said. "Where is he? How do you know he's dead?"

"Look, I saw him. Believe me, he's dead. Somebody

crushed his skull with a hammer. I practically stumbled over his body in that little room beneath the choir loft." I was getting to be an expert at this.

"I don't guess it would do any good to ask what you were doing in there," Shagg muttered as the four of us walked back to the old church. "Thought even you would have sense enough not to go inside a place like this alone."

"I left a message, didn't I? I waited as long as I could." I shrugged his hand from my arm. "What took you so long?"

He gave me a nasty look. "I don't have ESP. I had a few things to do before I got home, Jane. I only got your message a few minutes ago." He shook his head. "You really do need a keeper."

"Look, I'm sorry," I said, hurrying to keep up with his long strides. I had never seen Shagg so upset. "I guess I just wasn't thinking. I didn't expect to find . . . well, what I found." I let him walk in front of me. I didn't want to look at Dillard Moore again.

He gave my hand a forgiving squeeze. "You didn't say how you knew to come here. What's going on?"

"Miss Baby called. Said one of her students let it slip about a séance or something out here. All this stuff going on in the woods has her worried, and I don't blame her. I'm sure she must know Dillard's mixed up in it."

"Well, what did she expect you to do? Why didn't she call me? Why didn't she call the police?" Shagg lowered his voice. "Jane, are you sure it was Miss Baby who called?"

"Sure I'm sure . . . well, almost sure. Who else could it have been?" We had reached the sagging platform at the front of the church and I suddenly realized I couldn't bear to go any farther. The two teens lagged behind us, whispering to each other. I pointed to the tiny room where I had found what was left of Dillard Moore. "In there. He's in there."

Shagg brushed past me and opened the scarred brown door, then reappeared a few minutes later with an aggravated frown. "It's Dillard, and he's dead all right, but I thought you said there was a hammer."

"There is—on that old table against the wall, and there's blood all over the head of it."

"Well, it's not there now."

"What?" I started after him and stood in the open doorway, taking in the narrow room with one glance. The weapon was gone.

Chapter Eighteen

"I have the strangest feeling I'm in a science fiction movie," I told Shagg as we stood in the parking lot behind the police station—or at least Shagg stood; I leaned against a spindly honey locust that had sprung through the asphalt. "Now I know how these people feel who claim they've seen spaceships. Why won't they believe me?" I wiped sweat from my face with a dirt-streaked arm. Although it was after seven o'clock at night, the sun made my eyes feel hot and gritty, and heat rose from the black, oozing tar.

Police had gone out to the abandoned church to search again for the hammer, but I could tell from the way they talked to one another they didn't expect to find it. The two teenagers were still inside the station, giving their stories to a very stern detective, who looked as if he wished everyone were born middle-aged. Even Kristabelle's tears seemed to have no effect on him. I knew the girl hadn't seen the body, and Nathan wouldn't admit to it, although I suspected he had looked into the other room when he went back alone inside the building—which meant he had also seen the bloody hammer.

"Why would I lie about a thing like that?" I said. I broke off a frond of leaves and fanned myself. "Do they think I'm hallucinating or something?"

Shagg gave me a sad smile. "Well, you have had a pretty tough time of it lately . . . and let's face it, Jane, you did tell them sort of a wild tale last night."

"*Tale?* What do you mean, tale? Didn't they believe that, either?" I threw my makeshift fan to the ground and kicked it away. "The ashes in the pit were still hot, and somebody *had* disabled my car . . . and what about the dog? Shagg, they were going to kill that puppy."

"I know, I know. There's definitely something going on out there, it's just that—"

"Good Lord! They think I'm involved in it, don't they? Poor Jane! She's been through a hard time—practically got left at the church, you know. No wonder she's gone bananas. Well, I don't care what any of you think—something was wrong with my car last night!"

He reached for me, but I stepped away from him and ran to my car.

"No, Jane! Will you wait just a goddamned minute?"

I zipped out of the parking lot and left him standing there with a helpless look on his face. Let him follow me home! I hoped he would—so I could refuse to see him. I turned up the air conditioner full blast as I drove through town, deliberately running three red lights in a row. Shagg Henry was a man, wasn't he? Just like Jericho Scott and the up-and-coming young Doctor McCullough! Hurt one and they all bled.

My hands were shaking when I turned into Kennemore's Crossing, and I was surprised to see Eulonia Moody waving to me from her porch. "Guess you've heard about the sword," she said hurrying across the lawn to lean in my car window. "That Lovejoy boy has the same blood type as my Shelba Jean! The police just called here, said to tell you they found that hammer."

If it had been anybody else I would have hugged her. "Where?" I managed to escape into the relative shade of the screen porch. Eulonia followed.

"Somebody had thrown it over into the woods. Reckon they were in a hurry to get rid of it." Eulonia plonked herself onto the glider. "Said it looked like they were going to get a couple of good prints; don't guess they'll have to look far to find a match for them." She crossed her little black vinyl-covered feet. She was baiting me. I took it.

"And who would that be?" I asked.

"Why, that man that's been living there doing the yard work—the one you've been seeing so much of! You're lucky to be rid of that one, Jane Cannon. Cleared out, they say, but he won't get far."

"What makes you think Jericho Scott had anything to do with killing Dillard Moore? I'm afraid I don't see the connection, Eulonia."

"No, I guess you don't. Not many people would, but I happen to know he had good reason. That Lucas girl was his own niece, and everybody's saying she was carrying Dillard Moore's baby!"

"Are you sure about this? Who told you?" I didn't quite trust her, yet what she said made sense.

"Why, Miss Baby Kennemore! I called over there to see how she was—when I heard about Dillard, you know." Eulonia found a tissue in her pocket and dabbed the perspiration from her neck. "Not that I cared for Dillard Moore; we're well rid of him, I say, but he was Miss Baby's nephew and she must have had some kind of feelings for him. And the two of them did have words. Miss Baby said so."

"Who had words?"

"Why, Dillard, of course, and Jericho Scott! Miss Baby said she heard 'em out in the orchard in the middle of the night just a yelling and carrying on to beat the band!"

"About what?"

Eulonia rose with a sigh and left the glider sagging. "How should I know? I wasn't there."

After Eulonia left I sat for a full five minutes, letting reality sink in. As much as I distrusted Jericho Scott, I didn't think he was the head-bashing type; nor would he be so stupid as to leave his fingerprints on the murder weapon. It seemed to me as if the man were being set up. But why?

I scratched a chigger bite on my ankle. My clothes were streaked with dirt, my knee ached, and my stomach growled with hunger. Pizza and beer would set me straight. But the first thing I wanted was a long, hot bath.

The last thing I wanted was to see my neighbors Florence and Jeannette plodding up the front walk.

I hurried to meet them. If I could just keep the two outside, maybe I could get rid of them. Florence was upon me before I could open my mouth. "Well, I was beginning to think one of those freaks had got ahold of you for sure. Here it is almost dark, and you coming home to this big old empty house. We heard about your finding that Moore boy. Lord, that must've taken you back a plenty! Was he dead when you found him? Tell me —did you see who did it?"

I managed to shake my head. The spoken word would have been wasted on her. Besides, she probably knew more than I did. I tried to dodge the gangling woman as she followed me up the walk like a barking dog. At the front steps she flipped open the gold watch she wore pinned to her bony chest. "Why, it's almost eight o'clock, and I told Jeannette, I'll bet you hadn't had a bite of supper."

"Well, not yet, but I just got home. Look, I'd ask you in, but I really need to—"

"Mama only wants to help, Jane," Jeannette said accusingly. She stood in my path, hefty arms folded—as cushiony as a pink dimity airbag. "We've been worried about you. Why don't you come on home with us awhile? Calm down a bit; after all, you've been under a lot of strain. Why, I can see it right there in your eyes."

What she could see in my eyes was murder, but Florence came between us. "Never mind that," she said. "I want to know where your grandpa is. No telling what that old man's up to. And there must be a way to reach your parents—a phone number or something. I think they need to know what's been going on here, and I mean to tell them."

I stumbled backward into the azalea bed. This was a

good argument for gun control: If I'd had one, I would have wiped out the two of them and not thought twice about it. And where was Sudie? I didn't see her car, but she had been here when I called from the police station.

Jeannette shoved her round Cabbage Patch face into mine. "Tell me," she said, "was there very much blood?"

I steadied myself for the final siege. "Look, I know you—"

"What in the devil is all this blasted racket about? Can't a man get a nap around here?" Papa Sam stood in the doorway, stretching and rubbing his eyes as if he'd been asleep for hours.

"Well, look what the cat dragged in," Florence said, instantly deserting me. "It's about time you showed up. Where on earth have you been, Sam Lightbourne? You've got some explaining to do."

"Read it in the papers, Florence." My grandfather pulled me into the house and slammed the door behind us. "My God, that woman would make a preacher lose his religion!"

I buried my face in his chest and cried, clinging to his scrawny old shoulder as I had when I was a child, and loving the tobacco–shaving cream smell of him. "Where were you, Papa Sam? All hell broke loose after you left!"

"Here now! You didn't think I'd deserted you, did you?"

I shook my head and blew my nose on the crisp white handkerchief he offered. "But I've been worried about you. I didn't know where you were."

He laughed softly. "Had to see a man about a dog."

"Where?"

"First, I hear there's been some excitement around here. Maybe you'd better fill me in on what's been going on."

And so I did. After I soaked off my grime, the two of us sat on the screen porch in the dark, sharing a pizza between us and drinking beer straight from the cans. I stretched out on the glider facing away from Eulonia's gloomy house. I was glad I couldn't see Jericho's empty apartment from this side of the house, but like a cruel scar, I knew it was there, and would be there tomorrow and the next day to remind me of the man who had left in the night.

"They think Jericho Scott killed Dillard Moore," I said. "Eulonia says he's Etta Lucas's uncle and he and Dillard had some kind of argument yesterday." I waited for a reaction but got none. "He's gone, Papa Sam."

"So I hear." He took my hand. "Now, what's this about the Lovejoy boy?"

I told him about Nathan's ritual with the sword and how I had found it upright in the pentagram the day he disappeared. "At least the blood on it wasn't Shelba Jean's," I said. "Nobody seems to know where she is, but I think Jericho suspects more than he's telling."

Papa Sam sat silently while I told him about Eulonia's conversation with the motorcycle man and of my experience with the cult in the Widow's Woods. "If that cyclist hadn't distracted them, I don't think I could have gotten away."

Setting his drink on the floor, he stood and looked out at the street as I told him how the policeman was able to start my car on the first try. "I really believe they think I'm one of those crazy Satan worshippers, or that I'm going round the bend myself." I considered the last slice of pizza and decided in favor of it. "And sometimes I think they're right."

"There are more things in heaven and earth, Horatio . . ." My grandfather suddenly turned. "Be careful, Jane; just be careful. Things aren't always as they seem!"

His quote jolted me, made me sigh aloud, it sounded so much like Jericho Scott. I closed my eyes. I would have to quit turning to jelly every time somebody rattled off Shakespeare. I was glad it was dark. "That man on the motorcycle—he could've been the same man I saw at Eulonia's, the one who hums that awful hymn. And it sounds like he took Shelba Jean. For all I know, he may have killed her!"

"Oh, I expect Shelba Jean can take care of herself."

"You don't know this man! I've seen him—heard him.

And poor Eulonia! Papa Sam, she was hysterical." I shivered. "Just the sound of that motor gives me the creeps." And then I remembered the faint engine noise we had heard that afternoon at the abandoned church—a motorcycle going away, Nathan had said . . . *just before we found the hammer had disappeared.*

I stood and faced my grandfather. "You know something, don't you? Where have you been, Papa Sam? You were there last night, weren't you?"

"Well, let's just say I wasn't too far away." He patted my arm absently. "You'd better get to bed now, rest that knee. Reckon I'll give Cooter a call, let him know I'm back. You haven't seen him around, have you?"

I smiled as I went inside. "Tell Mr. Edwards he'll never get a job with Sam Spade," I said. Papa Sam obviously knew something, but he wasn't ready to tell me. Well, I would do some snooping on my own. While my grandfather was on the telephone I took a look at the small downstairs bedroom he always used. His worn leather traveling bag sat on the bed with an airline tag tied to its handle. I frowned when I read it. What in the world had Papa Sam been doing in Seattle?

I stuffed the filthy clothes I had worn that day into the laundry hamper, noticing the pink shorts I took off before going on my woodsy escapade the night before. Was it only last night I had found the note by my door and gone seeking help from the faithless Jericho Scott? *Note!* What had I done with the note? I scrambled through the pockets of the rumpled shorts.

"What's that?" Sudie came in as I unfolded the crumpled paper. She had been for a long walk with Nelson she said, and her face looked strained as she lay across the foot of the bed, covering her eyes.

"It's that note I found by the door last night—the one about Papa Sam being in the woods." I smushed the soiled laundry out of sight and slammed the hamper lid. "What's wrong? You look worried. Everything okay with you and Nelson?"

Sudie rolled over on her stomach. "I should worry. You're the one who found the body. Is this a new hobby or something?" She held out her hand. "Let's see that note."

I gave her the bit of paper and watched as she read it.

"This looks something like the one I got—the one I found on your door." Sudie snatched her handbag from the dresser. "I put it in here I think. Yeah, look—here it is!"

The paper was the same: a narrow, half page of pale blue, the kind of paper you buy by the pad, and the messages were both written with a black ballpoint pen. Only the handwriting was different.

Sudie looked over my shoulder. "I thought you wrote it. You'll have to admit, it does look kinda like your scrawl." I held the two messages in front of me. The notepaper was inexpensive, came in pastel colors, and could be bought just about anywhere. At first glance, the writing on Sudie's note did look like mine, and I could understand why she might be fooled. I folded the papers together to pass along to the police. The person who had left the messages was familiar enough with my handwriting to fake a passable imitation. It was not a comforting thought.

"Are you going to tell Papa Sam what we found out about the notes?" Sudie asked the next morning.

"Not in this lifetime. Let him find out for himself. He never tells me anything." I was delighted to have my grandfather back, but was relieved that he left soon after breakfast to go on about his business. The lumpy oatmeal and doughy biscuits he made and insisted that we eat sat like a wad of paste in my stomach.

Sudie wiped off the table for the third time. "Any special plans for today? Bodies? Black masses? Sacrifices?"

I laughed. "Well, I want to take those notes to the police and ask about the prints on that hammer." I poured another cup of coffee. It was the only decent thing my grandfather made for human ingestion. "Why do you ask?"

"Just curious. I haven't been to the Widow's Woods since—well, since we were kids. Would you think I was crazy if I asked to see where all that hoodoo took place?" Sudie ran steaming water into the oatmeal pot.

"If it were anybody else, no; but you, yes! I thought you were afraid of those woods . . . and you should be. It's not a nice place to be. There's something wrong there."

"Oh, I know it's dark and creepy and all that, but if we go in the middle of the day when the sun's bright, it shouldn't be so bad."

"It's more than dark and creepy; it's just plain—" I didn't know how to describe it. "Why do you want to go?"

Sudie shrugged, but she didn't turn around. "I don't know. Maybe I need more excitement in my life."

"Where were you yesterday? You would've been welcome to some of mine." I made light of her strange request, but I knew it must have something to do with Nelson Fain. "I'll make a deal with you," I said. "I'll give you a conducted tour of the woods, if you'll go with me first on a little visit next door."

Chapter Nineteen

"I don't know why I let you drag me here." Sudie said as we crept up the stairs to the old carriage house.

"Hush! Miss Baby might hear us. I just want to look inside." Shelba Jean Moody had to be somewhere, and it had occurred to me that Dillard Moore might have hidden her there after Jericho left. It didn't take long to find out the apartment was still unoccupied by anyone—living or dead.

I looked up at the fading red brick of Twin Towers, snaked with Virginia creeper. "Do you think she could be in there?"

"Wouldn't Miss Baby know?"

"Maybe. Maybe not. It's awfully big."

Sudie waited for me at the foot of the steps. "But if she's still alive, wouldn't she call out or something?"

"If she's able." I peered through a downstairs window into a dining room full of heavy, dark furniture. "We really should visit Miss Baby," I said.

Sudie looked at her watch. "But it's barely nine o'clock. What if she hasn't had breakfast?"

"Then maybe she'll ask us to join her." I linked my arm in hers. "Come on; it's the neighborly thing to do."

But Sudie dug in her heels, and I don't think I would

163

have budged her if Miss Baby hadn't come outside for the morning paper. "Are you girls looking for the police?" she asked. "They were dusting for prints in the carriage house, but they left almost an hour ago. I'm sure they made a grand mess in there."

So it was true: They suspected Jericho. "Miss Baby, I just wanted to let you know I'm sorry about your nephew," I told her. (How could my mouth say such a thing when my heart was screaming, "good riddance!") "Do they think your tenant had something to do with it?"

She ushered us inside. "That was my hammer, you see. He'd been using it to make some repairs." Miss Baby led us to a large kitchen that looked as if it hadn't been improved on since the forties. "Perhaps you don't know this, but Jericho Scott was the Lucas girl's uncle. He blamed Dillard for Etta's death."

I sat across from her at the chipped enamel table. "He told you this?"

"Well, he told Dillard, and Dillard told me. I'm surprised they didn't wake you last night yelling at one another." Miss Baby offered us a piece of cake from one of three that sat on the counter, and I felt a little embarrassed for arriving empty-handed.

"I realize my nephew was involved in things he had no business doing," she said, filling the kettle for tea, "and I won't pretend there was much love lost between us . . . but this—this—well, he didn't deserve this kind of brutality!" She set the kettle on a cold stove and sat down abruptly. "Jane, I would never have mentioned that old East End Church if I had known what you'd find. . . . I'm so sorry —believe me! Why, Dillard was supposed to be at work yesterday at some construction site way out in the country. Of course he never showed up."

I looked at her small, pale face. With a new hairstyle and some flattering clothes, Miss Baby wouldn't look any different from the ladies in my mother's garden club. I hoped she would be able to sell her land, vacation in Italy, and live as she pleased. I took a deep breath. The only way to find out was to ask. "Miss Baby, do you think your nephew had anything to do with Shelba Jean's disappearance?"

"I've thought about that—worried about it, actually—but no, I don't. They hadn't been seeing each other for several weeks now. I think Shelba Jean found someone else."

"Do you know who?" Sudie asked, but the teacher shook her head. "All I know is Dillard was quite upset at first; frankly, I stayed out of his way, but he was beginning to get over it. I'm afraid poor Dillard's romances were rather short-lived at best."

"Still, I think he was onto something," I said. "Something that happened in the Widow's Woods; maybe Etta's death had something to do with it. I don't know, but it's not safe around here, Miss Baby. I hope you're not staying alone."

She patted my hand. "Thank you, dear, but my sister's due in soon. That's Dillard's mother, you know. We've had a terrible time finding her. She and her latest gentleman friend were vacationing somewhere in New England. I'm afraid it's going to be a most distressing homecoming."

"A most distressing homecoming!" I repeated later that morning as Sudie and I pried about in the Widow's Woods. "Is that the understatement of the year or not? Poor Miss Baby! Her sister will probably blame her for Dillard's getting axed . . . or should I say hammered?"

"I think Miss Baby was born talking like that. Say, aren't we almost there?" Sudie looked over her shoulder and moved a little closer. Now and then she scrutinized the ground as if she were checking for something.

"Only a few more yards, just over that little hill." We followed the same route I had taken two nights before, and my knee began to hurt from the reminder of it. In spite of the pain, I walked a little faster. I didn't like being here any better in the daylight.

This time I stepped boldly into the circle where dead ashes and charred wood remained in the pit, surrounded by somber stones. The trees were a dark ceiling pressing down upon us, and I felt a chill, even though there was no wind.

Sudie shivered as she wove in and out among the stones, looking between them, behind them. "You're right; it's bad here, positively evil." But she kept on glancing about her.

"If you'll tell me what you're looking for, Nancy Drew, I'll help you search," I offered. But all I got was a blank look. We wandered into the fringes of underbrush, and I showed her where I had tumbled into what I had thought was a ditch. In the dim light that penetrated the thick foliage, I saw that it was, or had been, some kind of road —maybe a logging trail. Now it was overgrown with young trees and tangles of vines and brambles. I had fled to the right and what I'd hoped to be the safety of the main road and passing traffic. If I had turned left, I would have been stopped by a barricade of pines. It seemed to be the end of the path.

But today something made me go farther. "Looks like somebody's been through here," I said. "Seems to be some kind of trail on the other side. Let's see where it goes."

"Not me! I don't like the looks of it."

"You're the one who wanted to come here," I reminded her. "This must be how they've been getting away. Come on, it can't go back very far." I pushed through the foliage and found myself in a bleak passageway of saplings and interwoven vines that had grown up in the narrow ravine to create a natural tunnel. I jumped when Sudie clutched my shoulder.

"Don't leave me! I feel like somebody's watching!" she said.

The woods affected me that way, too, but I wasn't going to tell Sudie. A few steps farther I noticed we were no longer surrounded by living branches, but were entering a stone culvert with a faint light at the far end. "It looks like we're under what used to be a bridge," I said. "This thing must have been here forever!" I wished we had brought a light. The place smelled dank and moldy, and for all I knew could be crawling with snakes.

A tangle of bushes hid the exit. "Where in the devil are we?" I mumbled.

"Don't say 'devil!'" Sudie looked so serious I almost laughed. "What if some of *them* are about?"

"I don't think they like the daylight," I said. "Or is that just vampires?"

We stood in a desolate area of scrubby growth ringed by spindly pine saplings and trampled earth. It looked as if someone had dumped red fill dirt and attempted to smooth it about. Was somebody planning to build here? A crude makeshift road cut through the hills in front of us to a gravel thoroughfare to the east. Through a gap in the trees I saw a rusty silo, an abandoned tenant house with tumbledown chimney. "That's the old Randolph farm across the road over there," I said. "Papa Sam brought me here when I was little to watch them make sorghum syrup."

"Wonder who owns it now?" Sudie asked.

"Don't know—looks deserted. But I do know this is how those cultists have been giving them the slip. It's almost impossible to see past those trees, and I doubt if anybody knows about this back way in."

"Except the people who use it," Sudie reminded me.

I was glad when we emerged from the other side and found an easier path through the hillside, skirting the ceremonial site. I had come this way with Shagg when we followed Nelson Fain over a week before. The sun had a pale, filtered look here, as if it just didn't have the heart to shine, but a faint glimmer beside a rock at my feet caught my attention and I pushed aside ferns that almost hid it.

Sudie turned to wait for me. "What's that?"

"Looks like somebody lost their keys." I picked them up by the red plastic tag that said Odell's Garage. "Is this what you've been looking for?" I asked.

"Let me see those!" Sudie snatched them from me, but not before I saw the gold filigree pendant with the small emerald inset that hung from the ring. Apparently the keys belonged to Nelson, but the feminine jewelry seemed oddly out of place.

Sudie walked faster as she crammed the keys into her pocket. "Thank goodness! Nelson's been looking all over for these!"

"Somehow, Nelson just doesn't seem the type for delicate jewelry," I said.

"What?" Sudie was almost running now to where her small car waited in the bright sunshine.

I slid in beside her. "That pendant—or whatever it is hanging off his key ring—it looks more like something you or I might wear."

"Oh that? It's just a keepsake—sentimental trinket."

"Hmm," I said. "I've seen earrings like that somewhere. . . ." I almost bit off my tongue. I knew who had worn those earrings—Chloe Applegate! And that was exactly what was dangling from Nelson Fain's key ring. It wasn't a pendant; it was one of Chloe's earrings, the ones her husband had given her for a wedding present.

I rolled down my window and let the hot air blow in my face. I had seen Chloe wearing those earrings the last time I was home. Had that been before or after I saw her with Nelson in the park? I started to gnaw my last good fingernail. Afterward! I was sure of it because she had come over for a few minutes just before I left. I leaned against the scorching upholstery and closed my eyes. My knee hurt when I bent it.

Sudie looked at me and frowned. "What's the matter? You don't look too hot."

"That's just it; I am—too hot, I mean." I lifted the hem of my skirt and let the air billow beneath it. "Isn't your air conditioner working?"

"Conked out on me last week. I keep meaning to let Nelson take a look at it." Sudie flipped open the glove compartment. "See if you can't find something to fan with. I must have ten of those envelopes they give you when you go through the drive-in window at the bank."

Gratefully I grabbed the nearest one and waved it in front of my face. It didn't help. There was only one reason I could think of for Nelson Fain to have Chloe's earring, and the more I thought of it the worse I felt. Yet it couldn't have been Nelson who had written the two notes on blue paper if he had been with Sudie as she said. I had left the messages earlier with the police chief, who seemed to eye me with distrust and clammed up tighter than a skinflint's pocketbook when I asked him about the fingerprints.

Sudie stopped for a light. "Look, do you want me to drop you by the house? You don't look up to working today to me. Does your knee hurt?"

"Only when I laugh! No, that's okay; the store's cool and Alice is expecting me. I'll be all right if I can sit down awhile." And when I can get out of this car, I thought. A few minutes later I scrambled from the car and into the back of the shop, calling out to Alice to let her know I was there. In the small bathroom I threw water on my face and combed my hair, hiding my dust-smeared blouse beneath a smock. For a split second I thought of Jericho. Jericho would know what to do. But then Jericho had taken a powder. In spite of my irritation with him, I would have to call Shagg. Together we would work something out.

I added a touch of lipstick. My face had regained some of its color now that I was calmer. The empty envelope I had used as a fan lay where I had dropped it on the shelf above the sink, and I picked it up to toss away, absently reading what was on the front. The letter was addressed to Fred O'Leary of *The Sweetsprings Sun*, and the name C. Applegate had been typed in the upper left hand corner. The envelope was postmarked the day Chloe disappeared. If Sudie hadn't taken Chloe's column, she had been in the company of the person who had.

"Good heavens, you look awful!" Alice gasped when she saw me. "Where on earth have you been?"

I slipped the folded envelope into the pocket of my skirt. "Sudie wanted to ride out past the Widow's Woods, and her car's hot as Hades! Air conditioner's busted." I stood under the ceiling fan and closed my eyes. "Alice, who owns that old Randolph place now? You know, the one with the big silo?"

"Why that would be Barnette Henry—your friend Shagg's father—unless he's sold it recently. Why? You taking up farming?"

"Maybe. Have they found a way to grow money?" I was glad my back was turned. Shagg must have known about the other road! I knelt to compose myself, pretending to look for something beneath the counter . . . and if Shagg knew, how many others were in on it as well?

Since Alice took advantage of my being there to work with accounts, I had the front of the store to myself and was relieved that business was slack. I moved about mechanically, straightening boxes of shoes, dusting long-ignored crevices, grateful for the time to think. Just who *was* Nelson Fain? I had heard Chloe's married name, but the union had been so brief, I had almost forgotten the man existed. I thought the man Chloe married had been older, and his name wasn't Fain. The one thing I knew for sure was that Chloe had spent that period in Columbia. I threw the feather duster aside. Maybe Alice could remember.

Alice looked up from her ledger and frowned. "Chloe Applegate's husband? Let's see . . . it was a peculiar name—began with an S.—Shuttlemeyer? Stubblegate? No, *Stubblefield!* I remember Chloe joking about it; you know how she liked to go on! He was a distinguished-looking man, quite a bit older than she was."

"You met him?"

"Well, yes, at the wedding. And before that, too. Somebody gave them a party here." Alice smiled. "You were too young to be included then."

"Do you remember where he lived or worked? Anything?"

"He was connected to the university somehow . . . a professor, I think." Alice tapped a pencil on the desk. "Why? Surely you don't believe he had anything to do with Chloe's murder?"

I shrugged. "Why not? Isn't the spouse—or ex-spouse usually the most likely suspect?"

"I imagine the police have already thought of that," she said. "Besides, it's been an awfully long time."

Papa Sam told me the same thing. "Stay out of this, Jane. It's none of your business. Edwin Stubblefield and Chloe came to a mutual understanding a long time ago. The man wouldn't have a thing to gain by killing Chloe Applegate. Besides, he must be nearly as old as I am. I doubt if he'd have the energy to go around cutting off animal heads!" My grandfather paused. "Now, what about tonight? Want to come over and keep an old man company?" He sounded hoarse, like he might be coming down with a cold.

"I'm not sure, Papa Sam. I'll let you know." I smiled as I hung up the phone. Without meaning to, he had given me Chloe's former husband's first name.

Chapter Twenty

"**D**ean Stubblefield's office. May I help you?" The voice on the telephone was young and brisk.

I tried not to sound surprised. I hadn't expected a *dean*. What in the world was I going to say when I reached him?

But I was spared that decision because the dean wasn't in. She would be glad, the young woman said, to refer me to his assistant.

"Is there any way I can reach him at home?" I asked.

The voice took on a new tone—polite, but with undercurrents of disapproval. "Dean Stubblefield had bypass surgery only a few weeks ago and won't be back in the office for some time. If you'll give me your name, I'll be glad to refer you to someone else in the department."

"Oh, I'm so sorry! I didn't know. I live out of town and haven't seen him for a while." I didn't have to fake my astonishment. "And when did you say in went in the hospital?" I made a doodle on the telephone pad while nodding at a late customer. According to the woman on the phone, Edwin Stubblefield was undergoing surgery at the time Chloe Applegate was murdered.

When Alice left at five-thirty, I closed the door of the shop and tried once more to reach Shagg, but he still didn't answer and had switched off his answering machine. Before leaving I phoned the police to tell them about the escape route I had discovered in the Widow's Woods and was slightly disconcerted to find myself talking with the woman officer I had met two nights before.

"How's your knee?" Sergeant Totherow asked when I identified myself.

"Much better, thank you. I don't suppose you ever found out who was meeting out there?"

"From what the Lovejoy boy says, we believe it's mostly teens." The sergeant paused for a moment. "Look, Miss Cannon, if you have any idea where Miss Kennemore's tenant is, I hope you'll let us know. I probably shouldn't tell you this, but Jericho Scott's prints were found on the hammer that killed Dillard Moore."

"I haven't seen Jericho Scott since the day before he left," I told her. "But I'm not surprised his prints are on that hammer since he used it to make repairs.

"I know he's supposed to be Etta Lucas's uncle," I said when she started to interrupt, "but I really don't think he would take his revenge that way. Whoever killed Dillard must know this and is using him, and I think that person was still in the church when I found the body."

"You think he moved the hammer?" she asked.

"To make it look like Jericho was trying to hide the evidence. You'll notice, though, he didn't hide it very well! And when I first went inside that afternoon, I thought I heard somebody moving about. Probably the person who killed Dillard Moore."

"Then why didn't you say something sooner?" I could tell she didn't quite trust me.

"At the time I thought it might be mice, and then the two kids showed up. Frankly I'd forgotten all about it until now." I looked out the office window to an empty parking lot. Had whoever murdered Dillard been waiting for me?

"You seem to be in the middle of this for some reason or other," the woman said. "Any idea why?"

"Propinquity, I suppose. Or maybe I'm just lucky!" I had been asked that same question over and over the day before. I was tempted to hang up, but there was something else I wanted to know. "Do you remember if Chloe Applegate was wearing an earring when she was found? Gold with an emerald inset?" The day after Chloe's body was found police had drained the pool looking for clues. Maybe one had turned up there.

"I really don't know," the officer said, and her tone implied that she wouldn't tell me if she did. "Miss, we *are* here to help, you know. If anything else happens, call us first, please. And remember what I said about Jericho Scott."

Damn Jericho Scott! I wanted to spit him out like a rotten tomato. I hoped they tracked him down with drooling, snarling bloodhounds! So why did I protect him?

The flowers and Eulonia were waiting by my front door. I noticed the vase of roses first because they were bright red and cheerful, and eminently more welcome. Nevertheless, I hurried from the car when I saw my neighbor pacing the walk, apparently in a state of anxiety. She was dressed neatly in a navy rayon suit, shiny from wear, but clean, and wore a pink silk flower of dubious species pinned to her lapel.

"What's happened?" I asked. "Have you heard from Shelba Jean?" Eulonia was obviously dressed to go somewhere, but she didn't seem hysterical. I found myself pacing along with her.

"No, no, nothing like that, but I have to go away for a few days. I can't just sit here anymore! I have to do something. . . ." Eulonia made a slight whimpering noise as she dug in her handbag. There was something primitive about her actions that struck an ancient awareness in me, made me want to reach out. But not for long.

"Here." Eulonia slapped a key into my hand. "This is to my kitchen door. Repair man's due tomorrow to work on my washing machine. I told them to call you and you'd let him in."

"Sure, but why don't you come inside first? I could use

something cold to drink, couldn't you?" I started to put a hand on her arm.

"No time for that. Plane leaves in a couple of hours and I have to drive to the airport. Shouldn't be gone more than a few days. I'll let you know how to reach me." Eulonia got under the wheel of her gray sedan and started the motor. "You hold on to that key, now!"

I nodded. Eulonia's overnight bag, an ancient beige raincoat, and a black umbrella sat on the seat beside her. "Are you sure you don't want me to drive you?" I asked. But Eulonia didn't answer. She was already backing away.

Relieved, I picked up the flowers and hurried inside. There were thirteen of them and they smelled wonderful, but there was no card—not even the name of the flower shop. Since the town had only two florists, it shouldn't take long to find out, but it was after six; both businesses would be closed. I drew out a long-stemmed flower and held it to my cheek. Shagg! Of course it had to be Shagg. It was his way of making up for yesterday. I called his number again; this would give me an excuse to ask him about the Randolph property. But there was still no answer.

I fried bacon and sliced a tomato for a sandwich. Except for the sputtering of grease I felt marooned on an island of silence. This was Sudie's night to rehearse the hand bell choir at the church, so she wasn't expected until later. My grandfather was complaining of a cold, and when I had dropped by Papa Sam's earlier, he and Cooter were absorbed in a serious game of gin while absorbing a serious bottle of bourbon. I didn't think they would miss me. From my kitchen window I watched the dark canker of the Widow's Woods festering on the shoulders of the town. Each day they seemed to grow blacker, denser, closer, until I was afraid I would look outside one morning to find them just beyond my window.

It was not until I was cleaning up after my meal that I remembered the key. Eulonia's key. If Chloe had lost the filigree earring before the day she was killed, wouldn't

176

the remaining one be somewhere in her apartment? In spite of her laid-back demeanor, Chloe was organized; she had to be in order to run a nursery. If the earring were still there, it would be in its rightful place in the teakwood jewelry box she kept in her closet.

Eulonia's side of the house was even more cluttered than usual. Bills lay scattered on the kitchen table along with a half-eaten piece of toast and an almost empty marmalade jar. I started to throw them away, then changed my mind. Eulonia would know I had been inside the house.

The connecting door to Chloe's apartment was locked, but the key was in its customary place atop the molding. I was glad it was still light as I stepped into Chloe's stuffy back hall. My neighbor's belongings were just as she had left them, but Chloe's presence was gone: her laugh, her light, quick step, the elusive floral fragrance she wore. It was as if Chloe Applegate had never been in this place. The heavy oak stairs groaned as I climbed them, and I felt a salty tingling in my throat at the sight of the whimsical calico cat on the landing. My neighbor had painted the ceramic figure with one blue eye and one green eye after a pet she once had, and I hurried past it, glad to be in Chloe's airier bedroom where the late sun gentled the gloom.

It seemed disrespectful to violate the intimacy of someone's personal belongings, but I felt that Chloe would have understood. I fumbled in the darkness of the closet until my fingers found the smooth warm wood, and willed myself into a kind of false calmness as I brought the box into light. The earrings had a compartment of their own: cloisonne and silver, opal and turquoise, pink plastic cats, carved wooden beads . . . and one dangling gold bauble with a small emerald stone.

I touched it with the tip of a finger. I hadn't expected to find it here resting on its velvet indigo bed. This must mean that Chloe hadn't worn the earrings the day she was killed, and that Nelson Fain wasn't necessarily in-

volved in her murder. But how had he come to have its
mate in his possession?

I was in such a hurry to leave I was almost shaking as I
replaced the box on its shelf and tiptoed from the room,
hesitating at the top of the stairs. But why was I tiptoeing?
Who was going to hear me? Chloe's ghost? With one hand
on the dusty railing, I started down. That was when I
heard it—the sound of a footstep below. And it was a
footstep, there was no mistaking it. A solid, human footstep, and it seemed to be coming from Eulonia's side of
the house.

I clung to that railing as if it could keep out whatever
was on the other side. Should I go up? Down? If someone
should wander into Chloe's hallway, I would be in plain
sight. And what if they had heard me? Keeping close to
the wall, I slowly made my way to the bottom. I heard
drawers being opened in the downstairs bedroom
Eulonia used. She must have forgotten something. I stood
in the shadows at the end of the hall. If I tried to leave by
another exit, Eulonia would surely hear me. But what
excuse could I give? I would just have to make up something—say I'd heard a noise.

The noises stopped as soon as I stepped into Eulonia's
dim hallway, but I knew she was there, terrified no doubt
at discovering she wasn't alone. I called out to her but
received no answer. The door to Eulonia's room was
open and I paused on the threshold. "Eulonia, is that you?
It's me—Jane. I thought I heard somebody."

My only response was silence. And with painful awareness I knew it wasn't Eulonia in the room and that I had
given myself away. Someone stood in the corner by the
tall oak dresser, but I couldn't see his face until he
stepped into the light. And when he spoke I wanted to run
and to cry, and to my great annoyance, to laugh all at
once.

Jericho Scott moved out in front of me. "Jane! I'm glad
it's you."

My legs didn't seem to work. Neither did my mouth.
"What? How—how did you get in here?"

"Believe it or not, the kitchen door was open." He had letters in his hand. Letters that obviously didn't belong to him, and he had the effrontery to smile at me. "I had hoped for a more congenial meeting place . . . but then, here you are, and here I am!" He moved closer; if my arms were working he would be within slapping distance.

"Who was it . . . Schiller . . . who said there's no such thing as chance?"

Why, the fool actually thought I was going to stand there and let him shower me with his ridiculous quotations. I took a step backward. "Well, damn Schiller, and damn you! You can both go to the devil!" My words sounded every bit as mean as I felt. Good!

"I know I owe you an explanation, but I thought you understood."

"Understood what? Your leaving without a word? Did you think I was telepathic? And by the way, your 'novel' is repetitious!"

"But . . ." He groaned. "You obviously didn't get my message!"

"Obviously not. By the way, the police are looking for you—but I suppose you know that." I started down the hall toward Eulonia's kitchen. If I could get close enough to the door, I could dash outside.

I heard him following me. "Oh, God! You don't believe me, do you? I left a note in your front door. That old fellow—the one who follows you—was asleep on the porch, and I didn't want to wake him. Jane, I had to leave for a reason. I can't explain it now, but I will."

"Does it have anything to do with your little coven meeting in the woods?" I turned suddenly to face him. "You were just going to stand there and let them kill that dog, weren't you? And I was next!" I put a hand out behind me. The door was only a few steps farther. "I saw you driving by looking for me after I got away; I must say you're persistent."

With one startling step he whirled me about, placing himself between the door and me. "It was either the dog or you, Jane. I couldn't give myself away to save the puppy because then there would've been no one left to take care of you. I saw you back there following us. Some of those kids were so high on drugs, I didn't know what they'd do!"

I almost laughed. "Take care of *me?* What do you mean? I believe I did all right for myself."

"You put up a great struggle, but did you really think you sent that big guy sprawling with one shove?" Jericho Scott held up a bruised, raw knuckle. "To quote my mates the Beatles, you had a little help from your friend, Jane Cannon." He stepped aside to let me pass.

I wanted nothing more than to take that one step back into his arms and begin where we left off. Instead I moved a step away. I had been fooled too many times. "The police seem to think you killed Dillard Moore," I said. "And is it true that you're Etta Lucas's uncle?"

The silence that lay between us might have gone on forever if Eulonia's telephone hadn't rung. Jericho put a firm hand on my shoulder. "Don't answer it!" he said.

Chapter Twenty-one

I backed away from him, felt the weight of his hand slide from me. In two steps I crossed the room and snatched the phone from its cradle. It could be Shelba Jean calling for help.

"Eulonia? You don't sound like yourself." The voice on the other end of the line wasn't Shelba Jean's, but I thought I recognized it.

"Eulonia's not here right now. This is her neighbor, Jane Cannon. Could I take a message?" I faced him as I talked. If he took one step closer I would scream. I scanned the countertops, the table for a handy weapon, but except for the remains of her supper, Eulonia had put everything neatly away.

The caller hung up abruptly leaving a dial tone screaming in my ear. I was sure Jericho could hear it. He would know that no one was on the line. "How nice of you! I'm sure she'd enjoy it. You know which house it is, don't you? Fine. Then I'll look for you." My hand closed around the marmalade jar on the table; it left a sticky residue on my fingers and smelled of oranges. "That was somebody from the church," I said, hanging up the phone. "She's bringing over a salad." Could he tell I was lying?

Obviously. Jericho Scott pulled out a kitchen chair and plopped down laughing. "My God, Jane, you *are* an awful liar! Did you think I was going to charge over there and strangle you with the telephone cord? And please put that jelly jar down!" He placed both hands on the table. "See: I'm unarmed . . . and as innocent as a new-laid egg. I swear it!"

I washed my hands and wiped the jar at the sink. "It would really save a lot of time and worry if you'd just tell me what you want. Are you here because of Etta? And why have you taken Chloe's letters?" I sat across from him: two strangers at a kitchen table. We really didn't know one another at all, and I wasn't sure I cared.

"Yes, Etta Lucas was my niece—my older sister's child, but that's not my only reason for being here. And I didn't kill Dillard Moore!" Jericho looked at me across the table. His eyes wouldn't let me go. "Believe me, Jane, I'm not a member in good standing of that little woodsy bunch out there—especially after the other night. I let Dillard know I was interested, and he invited me to come along. I wish I could tell you more, but I can't. You're just going to have to trust me." His last words were barely audible, but they came at me full volume. "I do care about you, Jane."

I twisted the top on the marmalade jar and put it in the refrigerator. Please don't let him see my face! Don't let him see me cry! I rearranged the dishes people had brought over—many labeled with bits of tape—putting the jar on a shelf between what was left of Miss Baby's lemon chess pie and Ruby Lovejoy's bean salad. "Are you some sort of investigator, then?" The door of the refrigerator hid my face.

"You might say that." Thank goodness he hadn't moved, hadn't tried to touch me. "I don't suppose you got my flowers, either," he said.

"Flowers? When?"

"Why, today. I left them by your door myself—with a note. There were thirteen of them—one for each day I've known you."

I took a deep breath. The roses! And nosy Eulonia had gotten there first and read the message. Jericho's card had probably blown blocks away by now. I looked at him. Could I trust my voice? "The roses are beautiful, but I'm afraid Eulonia misplaced your note. She was waiting for me when I got home. She's gone off somewhere—looking for Shelba Jean, I think."

He nodded. "I don't suppose that was Shelba Jean on the phone?"

"No. She wouldn't tell me who she was, but it sounded like Cousin Myra."

"That's odd." Jericho straightened the stack of mail on the table. Eulonia had opened her phone bill and the lists of charges were scattered about. He made no pretenses about his curiosity, frowning as he scanned each one.

"Hey, that's really none of our business," I reminded him.

"There are two charges on here for calls to a number in Mullins."

"Then Cousin Myra must have gotten in touch. I'm glad."

He looked up at me. "Jane, these calls were made before we went to Mullins, before we ever met Myra Updyke."

"Maybe they're to somebody else." I reached for the phone. "There's one way to find out." Jericho stood beside me with the phone bill in his hand as the information operator gave the listing for Myra Updyke. The numbers were the same.

"That's strange," I said. "Why would the woman pretend she hadn't kept in touch with Eulonia? Why would she lie?"

"And what about Eulonia? Didn't you tell me she said she hadn't spoken with Myra in years?" Jericho put a hand on my arm. "Jane, since you came back here, Eulonia has gone out of her way to make people think you're—how shall I say it? Emotionally unstable. Haven't you noticed?"

I had noticed, but then Eulonia Moody always had a spiteful streak. "It's because of that man," I said. "The man on the motorcycle. She doesn't want anybody to find out about him, and it has something to do with what happened to Shelba Jean."

"Right. And I'm almost sure she was the one who splashed chicken blood on your porch."

"But why? How do you know?"

"To frighten you, I guess; get you out of that house. There was too much blood to have come from a prepackaged chicken. Whoever did it must have killed a live one to make it look that gory, and there's a woman out in the country who sells fresh eggs; runs an ad in *The Sun.* She said she sold a small fryer to Eulonia Moody the day all this took place." Jericho smiled at me. "What do you bet the Moodys had fried chicken for supper that night?"

I didn't think I would ever eat chicken again. Suddenly I had an intense desire to get out of Eulonia Moody's house. "Do you think all this has something to do with Chloe? Is that why you're here? But it couldn't . . . you came before Chloe was killed!" I saw Chloe's letters, tied with twine, bulging from the pocket of his coat. They looked like the ones I'd seen in her study the night of the intruder. "Those *are* Chloe's letters, aren't they? Where did you find them?"

"In Eulonia's dresser drawer wrapped in a flannel nightgown that must date back to the First World War." He patted his pocket. "Do you know where Shelba Jean's room is? Upstairs, isn't it?"

"Yes, on the front." I let him lead the way. I didn't want to go upstairs, but I didn't want to be left alone, either.

I wasn't prepared for what I saw. One wall of Shelba Jean's room was painted black, and a cluster of grim pen and ink sketches featuring people either dead or dying covered the space above her bed. As bizarre as they were, I felt compelled to take a closer look. The prints were well executed and mounted neatly on velvet. They could have been illustrations from Dante's "Inferno." In the center of the grouping a silhouette of a goat's head leered at me with burning eyes.

Jericho stood behind me, his hands loosely on my arms. "And the devil did grin," he said, turning away.

"Grin nothing! He's probably laughing his horns off! Look at this room: swastikas, pentagrams . . . and what are those funny-looking symbols? I'm worried about Shelba Jean!"

"The kid's on drugs." He said it so matter-of-factly I didn't question him. "Hard drugs, maybe, and who knows what else. I hope it's not too late." The symbols, he explained, represented letters of the Satanic alphabet, and the chant I had heard that night was the Lord's Prayer being recited backward. He stooped to study a framed snapshot on the table by the girl's bed; it was a small color photograph of a young man and a toddler building a sand castle at the beach.

I looked over his shoulder. The picture made me feel sadder than any of the Satanic emblems. "Must be Shelba Jean and her father. Pity . . . I think that's the only time I've ever seen her look happy." I turned to see Jericho looking through the girl's dresser drawers. "What are you looking for now?"

"Don't know. Probably won't know till I find it." Carefully he lifted out a box of costume jewelry, a cosmetic case, a curling iron, and a thin pad of inexpensive blue paper. It was the same stationery used for the notes Sudie and I had found at the door! I tore a page from the pad.

"Why are you doing that?" Jericho asked, and I told him. "That figures," he said. "Eulonia must have left those notes to get you and Sudie out of the way that night." He peeled off his jacket and threw it aside. "I'm roasting up here! See if you can open a window. I'll see what I can find in the closet."

His head and shoulders vanished into a curtain of acid-washed jeans as he searched the depths of the cubicle. I tugged in vain at the windows, but both had been painted shut. As I waited, fanning myself with an album cover, I happened to glance at the letters in the pocket of his cast-off coat. Should I? Definitely! Quickly I drew them out and took them to read by the window on the landing. There were three of them, mailed when postage was only twenty-two cents, and postmarked ten years before; and they were written to Chloe *Stubblefield* at a Columbia address.

My face grew warm and I felt like a shameless interloper when I realized I was reading extremely personal letters—love letters. The notes were by no means graphic, but were the tender idealistic ramblings of a young man very much infatuated. And the young man, I learned, was Nelson Fain! The third envelope contained two snapshots of a younger Chloe and a boyish-looking Nelson posing by what appeared to be a winding mountain stream with a picnic hamper between them. Chloe was toasting her lover with a wineglass while he gazed at her with an expression of utter devotion. The youthful Nelson wore glasses but no beard. Someone—Nelson, I supposed, had written on the back of one picture: "Thought you'd like to have these as a reminder of our day on Grandfather Mountain."

No wonder he had been poking about Chloe's apartment that night! He had been trying to find those letters!

"Well, I see you've helped yourself to the reading material." Jericho stood in the girl's doorway, the letterless jacket in his hand.

"Don't get self-righteous with me! I have as much right to see them as you do," I said. "Only I wish I hadn't! They must have had an affair while he was a student; maybe her husband was one of his professors."

"Looks that way." He held out his hand for the letters. "Do you mind?"

I noticed that he held a book at his side. "What's that?"

"Book on the occult, about six weeks overdue at the library." He flipped it open to reveal two letters. "And Shelba Jean's secret hiding place."

"Is that what you've been looking for?"

"Well, not really." Jericho groaned, handing me the letters. "Oh, go on! You'll manage to read them anyway. They're from Shelba Jean's latest love interest." But from the pleased look on his face, I knew that he had found what he was looking for, and it wasn't necessarily the letters.

The letters had been postmarked in June and mailed about a week apart from Myrtle Beach. "Kristabelle Douglas told me Shelba Jean met a new boyfriend when she went on the class trip to the beach last month . . . but then that's not really worthy of a news bulletin." I scanned a letter, not really wanting to digest its contents. Shelba Jean's latest, I found, was a lifeguard named Ross who had an unabashed lust for her and who misspelled every other word. From what I could make out, the two planned a romantic interlude sometime in the middle of the month.

"Do you think that's where she is—with this Ross? Would she really sneak away like that and make her mother think she was kidnapped—or worse?" Of course she would! The girl deserved black walls! I watched as Jericho put the letters back where he'd found them. The framed beach photograph, I saw, was missing from the table by the bed. "There's only one thing," I said. "Her car. She would never have left that new car."

Jericho stuffed Chloe's letters into his pocket as we left the room. "Just how far do you think they'd get in that Toyota? Eulonia would've had those two tracked down before the sun came up."

"But she's been gone for over a week! That's not right. Shelba Jean wouldn't give up that car this long for the sexiest lifeguard on the Atlantic seaboard!"

Jericho didn't answer, but Shelba Jean Moody was in danger. I knew it, and I think he knew it, too.

"I don't suppose you're going to tell me what you were doing over here," he said as we stepped outside into the muggy night.

He followed as I picked my way through tall grass to the gap in the hedge and my own backyard. Chloe had always kept the lawn trimmed, but Eulonia had other things on her mind. "I was trying to find serenity, I guess," I said. "And I thought I had—for a while." I told him of finding Chloe's earring on Nelson's key chain, and of its mate in the teakwood box. "So he must've had the

187

earring *before* Chloe was killed, or the other one would be missing, too."

"Unless he put it there himself."

"What? You mean—"

"Nelson Fain. You said you thought that was Nelson you saw in Chloe's apartment the other night. Maybe he was there to put the second earring back."

"Because the other one was still lost! I hadn't thought of that!" I sat at the kitchen table and stared at the vase of roses. It was after nine o'clock and Sudie had not come home. *Nelson Fain and Chloe!* It was hard to believe! Was that the secret Sudie guarded? Didn't she realize this man had probably murdered Chloe Applegate? Or maybe she didn't care.

"That awful night in the woods—the night I saw you there—my car wouldn't start. Somebody had done something to it—somebody who knows about engines! By the time the police came, nothing was wrong with it, so of course they didn't believe me. I wonder if it was Nelson . . . yet Sudie claims he was with her!"

"To give the devil his due, Nelson Fain isn't the only one who would know how to put your car out of commission. It's relatively simple to remove the distributor cap or loosen a wire. I could do it myself. Anyone could who knew the least bit about mechanics." Jericho looked up at the clock as he spoke. "I'd better clear out of here; I don't want to be around when Sudie gets back."

I looked up at him as he stood. "Just what makes you think Sudie *will* come back after what we've found out tonight?"

"And that's exactly why I'm leaving now," he said. And before I realized what was happening, he pulled me to my feet and kissed me with such feeling that I wasn't sure I was awake—or of much of anything else for that matter! And then he was gone.

Still dazed, I wandered out to the small front stoop where Eulonia and the flowers had waited earlier, and in a holly bush beside the steps I found the missing card from the flowers. Eulonia had tossed it aside after reading it, or the wind had carried it away. I flicked on the outside light and sat on the top step to read it.

Time will explain it all.
Thinking of you,
Jericho

I groaned aloud. Time would explain what? Why hadn't I received the note he was supposed to have left the night he disappeared? He had folded his tent in the dead of night as silently as any Arab, and now that he needed me again, the philosophical Jericho Scott was once more in my life, complete with roses and kisses and all that good stuff! Damn! If only I didn't enjoy it so.

I jumped to my feet with mixed emotions when Sudie pulled into the driveway. Somehow I was going to have to tell her what I had learned about Nelson Fain: his relationship with Chloe, his ransacking the apartment next door, and his obvious knowledge of engines. And then I remembered that a year or so ago, at Ralph's insistence, Sudie had taken a brief course in "powder puff" mechanics at the local technical college.

Chapter Twenty-two

"**G**ot any aspirin? My head's about to explode." Sudie kicked off her shoes in the living room and went to the kitchen for water. "Florence Gilroy has taken up hand bells! Good lord! She means well, I guess, but she just can't master the count. My ears are still ringing on the offbeat."

I hesitated. This probably wasn't the best moment to voice my suspicions. But then, there never is a suitable time to accuse someone's true love of murder.

"Florence said she hoped you were staying out of abandoned churches. Why, you couldn't pay her, she said, to go in that filthy place." Sudie made a face, then noticed the flowers. "Oh! Gorgeous roses . . . who sent them?"

Uh-uh, not now! I edged into the next room. The tale of Jericho and the roses would lead to Eulonia and Chloe and what I was doing in the house next door. Let the aspirin take effect. I pretended I hadn't heard.

"I wonder who else knew the kids planned a séance in that old church," I said. Had Miss Baby told anyone else? I decided to give her a call.

Miss Baby answered the phone with her name, as if she weren't exactly sure who she was—or why. "I wish now, of course, that I hadn't said anything," she confided. "But you seemed concerned, and I just felt as if I had to tell someone! Some of these children behave so strangely these days, I really don't know what to expect of them."

"Did you happen to mention it to anyone else?"

Miss Baby seemed to hesitate. "Well . . . I did say something at Eulonia Moody's that morning. Several of us dropped by about the same time. So sad about Shelba Jean. I'm just afraid something terrible's happened."

"Do you remember who was there?" I asked.

"Well, Eulonia, of course, but she never believes half you tell her. And the Gilroys—you know, Florence and her daughter. Then Ruby Lovejoy came in for a minute . . ." Miss Baby drew in her breath; she *thought* she might've said something to someone in the grocery store, but for the life of her she just couldn't remember who it was.

"You never did answer my question about the roses," Sudie said as I replaced the receiver.

Okay: *Now,* I said to myself, and told her. It was going to be a long night. "Why didn't you tell me Nelson had an affair with Chloe Applegate?" I said.

After a brief stage of indignant denial, Sudie turned to tears. "How did you find out?" she asked finally, looking across at Eulonia's dark house.

"It was the earring: the one on Nelson's key ring. I knew it was Chloe's."

"Look, I know it looks bad, but he had nothing to do with her murder, Jane, believe me. All this goes back about ten years or so when he was a grad student at the university . . . and yes, he did have a relationship with Chloe. She was warm and witty and exciting—you know what fun Chloe could be! And Nelson fell in love with her, or thought he did."

Sudie switched on the table lamp by the armchair, then switched it off again. "I don't guess many people know this, but Chloe's husband had some health problems soon after they married, and he became . . . well, impotent."

"And that's where Nelson came in!"

"You make it sound so nasty! But it wasn't like that at

all! Nelson really cared for Chloe; and he thought she cared for him."

"So, what was the problem? There's such a thing as divorce." I trailed a finger through the dust on the piano. Was I listening to a fairy tale? Other people had affairs, but not Chloe—not sensible, outspoken Chloe Applegate with her staid upbringing.

"It's more complicated than that," Sudie explained. "Chloe still cared about her husband; she didn't want to hurt him. To tell you the truth, I think she was a little in awe of him. Nelson said he was well on his way to becoming president of the university. And he was good to Chloe, too, gave her just about everything she wanted—"

"Except a sex life!" I blew the dust from my finger. "Still, that doesn't explain how Nelson came to have her earring or what it was doing in the Widow's Woods."

"Oh that!" Sudie's shrug belied her feelings. She was terrified and I knew it. It showed in every gesture, the timbre of her voice. "They met in the woods to talk," Sudie said. "It's out of the way—no one could see them there—and Chloe lost an earring; of course she didn't realize it at the time. Nelson found it after she left and put it on his key ring to return to her. And as he was walking around, giving her time to drive back to town, he found that circle of stones—you know, that place you showed me. He remembers putting the keys on a rock while he looked it over, but when he got ready to leave, they were gone. They must've slipped off, and he couldn't see them for the ferns."

"How did he get back to town?"

"Oh, he keeps an extra key wired beneath the truck. But when Chloe was killed, the poor man lived in fear that somebody would turn up that key ring and suspect him of her murder, especially after what happened before." Sudie looked down as she spoke.

"And the other earring?" I asked. "What about it?"

"What other earring? She only lost one. I guess she still has—had the other one."

"Sudie, how do you know this man is telling you the

truth? What was he doing meeting Chloe in the first place? After all, this affair—or whatever you want to call it—happened years ago! Chloe's been divorced much longer than she stayed married. Surely he hasn't been faithfully waiting all this time!"

"Hardly." Sudie brushed the hair from her face and looked away.

"He took Chloe's column from *The Sun,* didn't he?"

"What do you mean?"

I sat across from her. "Somebody called and tricked Fred O'Leary into leaving his office before he had a chance to read Chloe's last column, the one she mailed the day she was killed. Now it's gone—probably taken from Fred's desk—and whoever took it obviously thought Chloe was about to give him away."

"And you think it was Nelson? Well, it wasn't!"

"Then how did the envelope it was mailed in get into the glove compartment of your car?"

"What?" Sudie's head came up with a jerk.

"Coming back from the woods today, I used it for a fan. I can show it to you if you don't believe me." I watched Sudie's face as I spoke and saw bewilderment there.

"Then somebody must have put it there," Sudie said. "I didn't, and Nelson certainly didn't! Do you think I would've let you look in there if I thought you'd find that? It looks like somebody wants to make things worse for Nelson than they already are!"

I frowned. "Then who? Eulonia?" I told her about the notepaper and the chicken blood. "I'm sure she's read those letters, so she knows about Chloe and Nelson, and could have easily slipped something into your car."

"How do I know? Could've been anybody." Sudie moved to the piano and ran her right hand over the keyboard. I recognized the familiar chords to "Rescue the Perishing." "He should never have come here. Never!" Sudie brought her hand down with a crash.

"You're not telling me everything, are you? Don't you think it's time you let me know what's going on?" I hardly recognized my own voice. I sounded like my mother—or someone much older.

Her body sagged. "I suppose it's just a matter of time until everyone knows." She looked up at me. "You're right, there is more, and it's going to make Nelson seem the obvious suspect, but he didn't kill her, Jane! My God, the man's suffered enough!"

I stood behind her with my hands on her thin shoulders as if I could suffuse her with strength, if only I had some to spare. "Why? What happened? What did he do?"

Slowly and methodically Sudie closed the lid of the piano. "Ten years ago Nelson was convicted of rape. Chloe Applegate's testimony sent him to prison, but she lied, Jane. Because of her, an innocent man lost ten years of his youth and got a criminal record for life. And God forgive me, I hate Chloe for that!"

For some reason, I felt the need to make tea. I walked slowly into the kitchen, filled the kettle, and put it on the stove to boil. Sudie followed silently and sank into a chair at the table, burying her face in her hands. I found my mother's old brown teapot with the chipped spout. Its homeliness comforted me, gave me courage. "How long have you known?" I asked.

"Since a few days after Chloe was killed." Sudie looked at her fingers as if she'd never seen them before, then spread them on the table and examined them again. "I sensed something was wrong, but he wouldn't tell me what. I finally got it out of him that Sunday we went out. Remember? It was the same night you saw that man in Eulonia's kitchen."

I nodded, waiting for her to go on, then almost jumped out of my chair when the doorbell rang. Somebody pounded on the front door while jamming an insistent finger on the bell. Sudie looked from me to the clock with wide, frightened eyes. It was after ten.

"Don't worry. It's probably Papa Sam," I said. "He holds the record for impatience."

"I'm coming!" I called as I hurried to let him in. How

did he know when I needed him? After you brew tea—then what? I didn't know, but Papa Sam would.

"I called, but nobody answered, and then your line was busy, so I just came on over!" My grandfather strode inside with his giant steps and examined me at arm's length. His eyes were red and strained, and his voice sounded scratchy. "What is it, Jane? What's going on here?"

I pulled him into the kitchen where Sudie stood watching the kettle boil. Droplets of water hissed on the burner. "Am I glad to see you!" I said, getting out his special mug.

Later, over a second cup, Sudie told us Nelson Fain's story.

The spring before Nelson was to receive his masters degree, she said, Chloe's husband had come home unexpectedly from a conference and heard them together in his wife's room. The lovers heard him call out from below, but before they could think of what to do, Edwin Stubblefield was on his way upstairs.

There was no time to make a rational decision, and of course both of them were terrified. Nelson wanted to confront the man and accept the consequences, but Chloe wasn't ready for that. She convinced him to hide in an adjoining room until he could make a run for it.

Sudie traced the rim of her cup. "Nelson barely had time to grab his shoes and slip into the next room before Chloe started screaming. While her husband was trying to calm her, he bolted downstairs and out the back door. And he would have made it, too, if one of the professor's associates hadn't been waiting outside in the car."

I had to force myself not to laugh. It was all so vivid and reckless, like a ribald comedy. Across the table my grandfather frowned at me and sneezed. "Do you mean she let him go to prison for that?" He shook his head. "And I thought I knew Chloe Applegate!" he muttered into his handkerchief.

"She never would say who it was, I'll give her that," Sudie said. "Claimed he put something over her head and

196

she didn't see his face, but she didn't have to. Edwin Stubblefield's friend in the car identified him for her; and then, of course there was other evidence. Chloe gave her testimony in a closed session in the judge's chambers, and they kept it out of the papers." Sudie went to the sink and splashed water on her face. "Nelson Fain wasn't convicted on what Chloe said in court; it was what she didn't say that sent him away."

"And the man didn't even refute their story? Didn't try to prove his innocence? What kind of lawyer did he have?" Papa Sam slammed his mug on the table and sneezed again.

"Of course he did," Sudie said, "but by the time he realized what was happening to him, he was as good as convicted. Nelson thought Chloe would come through for him until the bars slammed in his face that last day, the day he was sentenced."

Papa Sam laced his fingers together. "And with the professor's prestigious background and Chloe's untarnished reputation, of course no one would believe him." He sighed. "I wonder if her husband did."

"He must have guessed," I said. "Their marriage didn't last too long after that."

"He made a generous settlement on Chloe, I hear," Papa Sam wheezed. "Maybe he felt he was well rid of her." He got up to put the cups in the sink, touching Sudie's shoulder as he passed. "Well, I'll see what can be done tomorrow. Not much use in worrying any more about it tonight."

I agreed. It was after eleven, he needed his sleep, and my knee was beginning to hurt again. I took two aspirins and a quick shower and crawled gratefully into bed, after convincing Sudie to do the same. Poor Sudie! I watched her lying stiffly on her side with her face turned to the wall in the bed across from me; I doubted if she slept at all that night. Were men worth all the trouble? Just where did Jericho Scott go in such a hurry when he left earlier? And where had he been the rest of the time? And then I stopped wondering and slept.

• • •

The next morning police arrested Nelson Fain for the murder of Chloe Applegate.

Sudie scarcely spoke and moved about like a sleep-walker all day. I didn't like the look in her eyes. She was not allowed to see Nelson, at least not for a while, and I was glad. If Nelson Fain were as loving and caring as Sudie made him out to be, seeing her would only add to his worries.

Was Nelson mixed up in the murder of Dillard Moore? I couldn't see any connection between the two; and I didn't know if he had been out of prison long enough to have killed Etta Lucas, or why he would have done it. It just didn't make any sense.

But he did have a motive for killing Chloe. Nelson wanted to clear his name, and had come to Sweetsprings to reason with her, convince her to come forward and admit their relationship, or at least let him have the notes and pictures for evidence. And according to Sudie, Chloe was seriously considering the request. Surely her conscience must have bothered her.

But suppose she had denied his entreaties? Chloe enjoyed her station in life: the independent, respected community leader; admired nursery school director; and member in good standing of the Sweetsprings First Baptist Church. Her weekly column guaranteed her an invitation to just about any social gathering in the area, and her closest friends, although not necessarily wealthy, considered themselves the town's social elite. No, I thought, Chloe wouldn't have wanted to give that up without a struggle. And I could understand why Sudie hated her so. Had she hated her enough to kill her? Sudie claimed she'd learned of the relationship after Chloe's death, but I had only her word for that.

I was appalled at my own musings. This was Sudie I was thinking about. My Sudie. The same friend who pulled me through high school algebra, who suffered with me over my traumatic breakup with Mac. And if I knew where to find a hair shirt I would have worn one.

Somehow we stumbled through a day that seemed ten years long. I left Sudie only for a few minutes to make sure Papa Sam had a supply of lemons and whiskey and found him enjoying poor health, but Jericho called while I was gone. "Said he'd call back tomorrow," Sudie told me with a fragment of a smile. If only she knew that in all likelihood, Jericho had been the one who was responsible for Nelson's arrest. I still didn't know who he was working for, but I was almost certain he had gone to the authorities with information about Nelson's affair with Chloe.

That night Sudie slept downstairs on the sofa. "I don't want to keep you awake with my tossing," she said. "And maybe the television will eventually lull me to sleep." I had trouble sleeping, too. With death and sorrow on either side of us, it seemed the whole neighborhood of Kennemore's Crossing was bogged down in misery.

It was the smell that woke me. The strong, acrid smell of gasoline that burned my nostrils and made me vaguely sick. I went to the window. Was somebody siphoning gas? But the smell was coming from inside the house—from somewhere downstairs! Barefoot and robeless, I called to Sudie from the landing but got no answer. Snatching a towel, I covered my face and hurried downstairs, my eyes smarting from the sting. By the eerie gray light of the television test pattern, I saw the covers thrown back from the sofa and Sudie's crumpled pillow on the floor. The pungent smell of fuel permeated the room, and I fumbled about in the darkness, trying to find its source.

It was stronger in the kitchen, and when I turned on the light I saw why. Pools of oily liquid covered the floor and snaked in a glistening stream under the table. I threw open the back door to the dark night air and called again for Sudie. But Sudie Gaines wasn't there.

Chapter Twenty-three

Fire! All I could think about was fire. Someone had meant to toss a match into the center of all that gasoline and burn down the house with us in it! But who? And why? Sudie had obviously interrupted him, but where was she now?

I mopped frantically at the smelly fuel with old towels and anything else I could find. One tiny spark would turn the whole place into a conflagration, and whoever had planned it might still be around with a handy lighter. (Welcome home from England, folks . . . sorry about the house.) Even with all the windows open and the fan working overtime, the fumes made me dizzy as I washed away the residue.

The police came as I was wringing out the mop, the same two who had rescued me from the roadside a few nights before. The woman officer spoke slowly and calmly, as if she were dealing with a child, and I knew I must have sounded hysterical when I called. The three of us moved outside to get away from the strong smell, and I felt as if I were walking into smothering black wool.

The policeman called Leland took a notepad from his pocket. "Now this friend of yours—the one you say is missing—hasn't she been seeing that man they arrested?

That guy who worked up at Odell's? Do you have any idea where she might have gone?"

"Look, you don't understand!" I wanted to grab him by his collar. "She hasn't *gone* anywhere. Somebody took her, and if we don't find her soon, it could be too late." I looked at Eulonia's empty house; on the other side of us the dark hulk of Twin Towers seemed to watch through shuttered windows, and the black woods above us appeared to have crept even closer. For a moment I felt a peculiar chill, and I knew without a doubt that—human or not—something, or someone, bad in the basest sense, was not far away.

Sergeant Totherow stuck her head into the kitchen and sniffed. "It's still pretty strong in here. Why don't you wait here while we look around? If somebody's inside, we'll find him."

But no arsonist hid inside our house, nor was there evidence of a prowler at the Moodys'. Yet somehow I knew he was near.

"We'll be glad to drop you off somewhere," the woman offered before they left. "I don't expect you'll want to stay here tonight—with or without gasoline fumes."

"Thanks, but I have my car. You will let me know if you find Sudie?" I stood in the doorway and watched them back away. Did they really expect me to sleep tonight? Inside I looked at the clock for the first time since the stench of gas awakened me. It was after three in the morning. I changed the robe I had thrown on earlier for shirt and jeans and grabbed the first pair of sneakers in my closet. I had to find Sudie!

I hesitated by the telephone. Papa Sam's cold was still in its sit-up-and-take-light-nourishment stage, and his condition hovered somewhere between abject suffering and death. And I had no idea where to find Jericho Scott. The Moody house looked as if no one had ever lived there. Eulonia had never called, and probably never meant to. The police had tried to rouse her before checking her doors and windows for signs of forced entry, but were met with no response. I didn't care if she never came back, but in spite of all the mean things she'd done, I hoped she'd find Shelba Jean. The key to Eulonia's kitchen door was still on my dresser where I'd left it. I was alone.

Under different circumstances I would have taken sadistic pleasure in waking Shagg Henry in the middle of the night, but this time his grumpy, mumbled greeting made me want to cry with relief. And after I told him what had happened he was instantly awake and came skidding into my driveway only a few minutes later.

He was solid and warm and familiar, and I'd never been as happy to see him. "Shagg, I'm scared," I said as I slipped gratefully into the seat beside him. "We have to find Sudie—soon! Whoever meant to set that fire didn't expect her to be sleeping downstairs. She must have frightened them away, but then what? Do you think there could have been more than one?"

Shagg didn't answer until we had reached the end of the block. "Now, don't get upset with me for saying this, Jane, but you'll have to admit our Saint Sudie hasn't been herself lately. All this infatuation with that mechanic at Odell's—how do we know he didn't kill Chloe?" He barely paused at the stop sign, then zoomed full speed ahead. "With all that's been going on, I wouldn't be surprised if Sudie didn't pour that gasoline there herself."

"I can't believe you said that!" I braced myself against the dashboard. "Just shut up and drive, okay?"

He shifted into second and gunned up the hill. "Sure thing."

"And slow down, will you?" It occurred to me that I didn't know where we were going, so I asked.

"Sudie's, where else? Jane, she might not realize what she's done, might not even remember it, but I have a feeling Sudie's back in her own bed sleeping like a baby."

"Do you think you might explain what you're talking about?" I said.

"Remember how Sudie's parents died? There was a fire, a house fire when she was four or five. She told me about it once."

"I didn't think she remembered, but she didn't start that one."

"No, but her parents died getting her out, and her grandmother never let her forget it. That's a heavy load to lug around. Now, with all that's been happening . . . well, this isn't a surprising reaction!" He jerked to a stop beside Sudie's dark apartment.

Oh, give me a break, Shagg! I thought. Everybody knows you majored in psychology! But I didn't say a word as we went inside, using the key Sudie had given me. And after what he had said, I was almost relieved to find the place empty.

"Now where?" I asked as we got back into the car. "And what made you say such an awful thing? You know Sudie would never hurt me or anybody else!" I tried to control the anger in my voice. "She's been through a lot with Nelson's arrest. She really does love him, you know."

Shagg laughed faintly. "What do I know about love? It's all just a comedy of errors if you ask me."

And minored in drama, I thought; but again, I didn't say it. He sounded so tragic I picked up his hand and squeezed it. "Don't worry; we'll all live through it. I did!" I looked at him beside me, his arm draped across the steering wheel, his face expressionless. "Why are you acting this way? Shagg, what's happening to you?"

"Oh God, I wish I knew! No—no, I don't mean that—I don't want to know!" Shagg covered his face with his hands. "In a way I was hoping Sudie was involved. It would've been so much easier. Jane, I'm afraid I've made a horrible mistake."

"About what?"

"Eulonia. It must have been Eulonia! Why couldn't I have seen that?"

I turned my face aside. "Shagg, I need your help. Please don't let me down now." I didn't raise my voice; I didn't have to.

"That man you kept seeing—the one who rides the motorcycle? Calls himself Elias Hawkins, but he's really Aaron Moody!"

204

"Eulonia's husband? But Aaron Moody's dead! He was killed in a construction accident."

"That's what the insurance company thought. What Eulonia thought until he turned up about a year ago. Aaron Moody's alive, Jane. I saw him for myself, and he's taken Shelba Jean."

"Taken her where?"

He shook his head. "I'm not sure. She's with some of his relatives up in Washington state, I think. When her father saw what she was into, he took matters into his own hands."

"And Eulonia wants her back?"

"Naturally. Eulonia doesn't let go of anything that be- longs to her —especially money. Now she's afraid some- body will find out about Aaron and make her give back the money she got when he 'died.'"

"Do you think Eulonia killed Chloe because she found out? What about Dillard Moore?" I found myself clutch- ing Shagg's shoulder. "She couldn't have poured that gas- oline there. She left yesterday to try to find Shelba Jean and hasn't come back."

"How do you know she hasn't?" The car lurched as he spun away. "Oh God, I hope we're not too late!"

"It's all right; take it easy, Shagg." I would have touched him, but that seemed to trigger his erratic behavior. "Just slow down a little, okay? I want to be in one piece if— when we find Sudie."

Familiar scenes whizzed past in a blur of trees and houses as Shagg maneuvered the streets of Sweetsprings as if he were on a racetrack. I felt like a participant in an old black and white movie, hurtling toward the cliff while the music soared to a violent crescendo. Any moment now the hero—or someone—would save me.

Tires squealed as Shagg turned the corner, not even bothering to slow for a light, and the car veered as he swerved to avoid a cat. I hung onto the door grip and faced him. He looked colorless in the predawn light. His pale skin, grim mouth, the tense set of his jaw created a gray silhouette. I was afraid of what he might do. But no hero was going to come along and save me. I would have to save myself. "Damn it, Shagg Henry," I said. "Either slow down or let me out right now! I don't want any part of your stupid death wish."

He didn't answer, but he did ease up on the accelerator. I let my breath out slowly. "I'm to blame for this mess," he said.

"What do you mean?" In the dreary light I saw the wet streak on his cheek, the tightness of his fists on the wheel. "Tell me, Shagg. What kind of trouble are you in?" I felt the small car vibrate with the growl of the engine. "It has something to do with the Widow's Woods, doesn't it?"

Shagg leaned over the wheel. "If I'd only said something, Chloe might be alive today."

I tried to fight the queasiness that rose within me when I saw where we were going. The Widow's Woods loomed like a dark green fungus in the distance. "About what?" I asked.

"About what happened to Etta." He glanced at me. "Etta Lucas was pregnant with my child."

"Oh, Shagg, Shagg! You didn't—"

"No, I didn't kill her, Jane. She was alive when I left her —I swear it! It must have been Eulonia. Oh God, I should have said something long ago."

I closed my eyes, waited for him to go on.

"We went to the woods to talk that day," he said. "It was quiet there, secluded. I wanted to marry Etta, make a home for her and the baby, but she had made up her mind to get an abortion—it was her body, she said! Hell, it was my baby, too, but I couldn't talk her out of it."

"What happened?"

"Nothing. We argued. I said some things I wish I hadn't said . . . and she ran away from me—said she never wanted to see me again." His voice seemed to catch in his throat. "I left her there, Jane; I shouldn't have left her alone, but the dog was with her. I thought she'd be all right.

"As I was leaving I saw Eulonia. She had parked her car off the main road and was standing outside of it, talking to that man with the motorcycle. I nodded to them as I passed—wasn't in much of a mood for good fellowship —but I couldn't avoid them."

"You were on foot?"

He nodded. "Less noticeable than taking a car. I was Etta's high school counselor—remember?"

"But how did you know he was Aaron Moody?"

"I didn't at first, but she acted so strange—I could tell she was uncomfortable about my seeing them together. Of course then I didn't give a damn about anything! If she hadn't reminded me of it, I'd never have given it another thought."

I looked up at the hills around us and felt the cold. I wished I had brought a sweater. "Do you think she killed Etta?"

"It makes sense. Etta had to have seen them. Maybe she made the mistake of asking questions." He paused. "The next day—after they found her—Eulonia came to me. She knew Etta was pregnant because Eulonia worked in the drugstore where Etta had her prescriptions filled. It didn't take a Ph.D. to figure out I was the prospective papa! She told me how Aaron had turned up wanting to be a part of Shelba Jean's life, and made me swear not to tell anyone I'd seen them together. In exchange, Eulonia promised she'd keep my secret about the child Etta carried."

"But you didn't suspect her of murder?"

"Not then. Why should I? It was all the things that happened afterwards that made me wonder. At first I just thought she was crazy-scared like I was." He sighed. "Now I just think she's crazy!"

"That day in the post office, it was Eulonia, wasn't it? She was the one who sent you that candy wrapper?"

He nodded. "I must've dropped a few after I left Etta. Eulonia picked them up—kept them." He made a faint noise, a kind of moan. "After that, any time she wanted to threaten me, make me do something, she'd mail me one of those things!"

I knew what was coming, but I had to ask. "Like what, Shagg?"

"Like sprinkling that chicken blood on your porch."

"And . . ."

He just looked at me. "Isn't that enough?"

Chapter Twenty-four

"**B**ut why?" I pressed my hands to my face. They were icy cold. "What have I ever done to Eulonia Moody?"

"You were too close, and asking too many questions. She wanted to scare you away." He didn't look at me. "And when that didn't work she tried other methods."

"Away from what? Oh God, Shagg! That wasn't you in my room that night?" I trembled at the memory of it. Those eyes.

He did look at me then. "When? You mean the night you saw the widow? Of course not! And I did lock those doors. I don't know how anyone could get inside."

"Do you think it was Eulonia?"

"She says not. Positively denies it, and I believe her. Frankly, I don't think Eulonia has that much imagination! And Sudie's grandmother had one of her crying fits and she spent that night with her. It couldn't have been Sudie, and it certainly wasn't me." Shagg looked aghast at the thought. "Who else could it have been?"

I stared at the narrow road ahead. I could feel the presence of the woods. Waiting. "What other methods?" I asked. My voice sounded like a child's.

Shagg slowed, looking for the turn. "What?"

"Eulonia. You said she used other methods."

"Jane, Eulonia was the one who did that to your car. She took some kind of course last year, a mechanics class for women. My mom was in it with her—Sudie, too, I think."

I told him about the blue notepaper we had found in Shelba Jean's room. "But why would she go to all that trouble just to get me out of the way?"

"She thought you knew where your grandfather was. She needed to get you and Sudie away from the house long enough to see what she could find—a letter, phone number, anything!"

"My grandfather? What does Papa Sam have to do with it?"

I didn't think he was going to answer. "I'll let him tell you that," he said at last. "But Papa Sam knew about Shelba Jean all along, Jane. I think he had something to do with her being where she is."

"And Eulonia knew this?"

"I think so. And when Eulonia couldn't scare you off, she tried to discredit you—make people think you were kind of, you know, balmy."

My stomach lurched as we turned across from the old Randolph farm and bumped along the weed-choked road. I fumbled with my seat belt. Was Eulonia's secret worth murder?

Shagg stood beside the open car door, waiting. "Somebody took Chloe's last column from Fred O'Leary's desk," I said. "I don't suppose you'd know anything about that?"

He shook his head impatiently. "You can't blame that one on me!"

"You didn't put the empty envelope in Sudie's car?"

He switched on a flashlight and led me across that bleak, clay-filled area and into the tunnel, pushing aside the overhanging foliage. "What envelope? When was this?"

I didn't answer. It must have been Eulonia. After finding Nelson's letters to Chloe, she wanted to throw suspicion onto Sudie. Anyone seeing the envelope in the glove compartment would naturally think Sudie had something to do with stealing Chloe's column . . . and ultimately with her murder—just as I had! I rubbed my burning eyes as I followed Shagg through the damp stone culvert. If only we reached her in time.

Abruptly Shagg stopped to listen, holding me back with one hand. On the hill beyond us twigs snapped as someone walked about.

"You knew," I whispered.

"Shh!" Shagg switched off the flashlight. "Knew what?"

"About the other way in—the tunnel."

"Of course I knew. The police showed it to me yesterday. It's just across from some of Dad's property, you know. This is how they've been getting away.

"Wait here," he said as we came out onto the old logging road. "Let me see what's going on. If I don't come back in a few minutes . . . well, maybe you'd better go for help."

"Okay," I said. He gave me a parting touch and moved away from me. I heard the swish of his feet through the foliage as he climbed the hillside. A clod of dirt crumbled, fell. Still I waited. But when he shouted Sudie's name, I started after him, running.

In the gloom of dawn I saw the three of them: Shagg, motionless at the edge of the clearing; two other figures stood inside the ring of stones—or one of them stood, bound hand and foot to a sapling. The other circled her, pouring gasoline in a ring. The smell hung low in the air, wrapped us in its oily vapor.

The captive spoke, tossing her head from side to side. "Please, somebody stop her! She's completely lost her mind! Stop her before she burns us all alive."

I reached out in the darkness and found Shagg's hand. He pulled me close to him. It was Miss Baby!

"Isn't that what you meant to do to Jane and me?" Sudie set the can of gas at her feet but she held a box of kitchen matches in her hand. I heard them rattling. "She killed Chloe, you know—Dillard Moore, too—her own nephew! She admitted it! And she was going to get rid of us as well, weren't you Miss Baby?"

I took a step forward. "Sudie . . ."

"Get back, Jane! She deserves to die! She's evil—like these woods—like the widow!" A match flared in the darkness. "Shagg, make Jane go away. Both of you, go away."

"All right. But first tell us what happened. That's right, let the match go out. We have time." I watched the frail light shiver and die. Had Sudie gone completely crazy? It looked like Shagg was right; we had to help Miss Baby! If only we'd left a message, someone might come. "We were worried about you," I said. "We didn't know where you were."

Sudie took out another match, but she didn't strike it. "I was almost asleep when I heard her," she said with a quick glance at her captive. "I think it was the smell that woke me. Anyway, she ran, and I followed her around by the pool and through the orchard. At first I thought it was Eulonia, but then I got a look at her face. I must have made a noise because she was waiting for me on the other side of the carriage house, and she had a gun."

Miss Baby made a weak attempt to laugh. "Oh, surely you don't believe her. The woman's obsessed with fire, remember how her parents died. . . ."

But her words faded as Sudie slowly circled the tree. "I must have been in shock," Sudie said. "I couldn't believe it: Miss Baby Kennemore! Sweet, harmless Miss Baby! She held me there until she saw the police leave, locked me in a storage room, and poured gasoline under the door. If I made any noise, she said, she'd set fire to it!"

"Can't you see she's crazy?" Miss Baby whimpered. "Do something! Make her stop!"

Again Sudie struck a match, and this time she held it until it almost burned her fingers. "After the police left," she said, "she made me drive her here. I think she meant to kill me—make it look like a sacrifice —then come back and finish what she started." She looked at me and tossed the match aside. "You were meant to be next, Jane.

"But she slipped climbing up here and I managed to get

the gun away. Now the roles are reversed! How does it feel, Miss Baby?"

I felt Shagg tensing beside me, and put a warning hand on his arm. "Did you kill Chloe, Miss Baby?"

She frowned at me as if I'd spoken out of turn in class. "Don't be ridiculous, Jane."

"Tell them the truth, Miss Baby," Sudie said. "Tell them what you told me!" She shook the box of matches and took out a third. "And tell them why."

Still the woman looked back at us. She had lost her glasses and there was a smudge of dirt on her cheek. She was silent for so long I thought she was never going to speak, but Sudie stared her down. With one flick of her fingers she could set the whole place on fire, and Baby Kennemore knew it.

"It was because of Etta," she said at last. "Poor little Etta. She thought she was doing me such a favor. Of course I had no idea the child was . . . in the family way."

Shagg uttered something under his breath and started forward, but I grabbed his arm. "She saw it, you see. She would've told. I couldn't take the chance."

"Told what, Miss Baby?" I asked softly.

"Why, about those chemicals! And don't pretend you don't know! I heard Dillard talking to you the other day! Don't you think I was aware of your poking about out here? You knew what was buried in these woods."

I looked to Shagg for help, but his eyes were on Miss Baby. "So that's why there's all that fill dirt across from the Randolph place," he said. "What's under there, Miss Baby? What kind of chemicals?"

"Oh, I don't know! Some kind of thing the power companies need. PCB or something! It's used in insulators for transformers. They paid these people to get rid of it, but they ran out of places to put it, so I let them bury it here."

"That's illegal, isn't it?" Sudie looked at Shagg.

"It's my land, isn't it?" Miss Baby's voice rose. "How could I know somebody would come along and want to develop it? And they paid in cash, too—a lot of cash! I spent the whole summer traveling! Nobody would ever know that stuff was under there if it hadn't been for Etta Lucas and that dog of hers!"

"It had been raining hard all week," Shagg said. "Must have exposed some of the drums."

"She came by my house to tell me," Miss Baby said. "Said she thought I ought to know. Of course I thanked the child. Where? I said. Show me where, and she did."

"And that's when you killed her." Shagg's words were flat. Hopeless. "How?"

"Piece of heavy wood . . . she never knew it, I promise. But that little dog just about chewed my arm off, so I had to kill it, too. That's where I got the idea to make it look like a ritual thing. I knew a little about that from Dillard. Then, after it got dark, he brought over some dirt from the construction site and covered up those chemical containers." Miss Baby smiled at us. "Now look, there's going to be enough money for all of us. This land developer made a generous offer—more than I ever dreamed! All I've ever wanted is to travel. Just tell me how much you want and no one need ever know."

"What about the people who buy land here?" I asked. "Won't that stuff get in their water supply?"

"Oh, for heaven's sake, Jane! Not unless those containers leak. Besides, that's their problem, isn't it?"

Sudie's hand was shaking. "I don't understand. Why did you kill Chloe?"

"Well, my goodness, dear, I had to." Her voice was matter-of-fact. "Chloe suspected something was wrong; why, she even mentioned it in her column—something about secrets buried in the woods. It was only a matter of time before she made it a matter of public knowledge!"

"But Chloe was afraid of water," I said. "What was she doing at your pool?"

"Looking for that cat. Of course I'd already killed it by then, but I called and told her I'd seen it there. She was such a fool about that animal!" Miss Baby looked up at me, but I don't think she saw me at all. "And I was waiting for her," she said. "You weren't supposed to be at home, Jane. No one told me you had come back."

Chloe must have noticed the oddly-placed fill dirt when she went there to meet Nelson Fain. "Then you were the one who took her column from *The Sun*?" I had to know.

She attempted a smile. "Well, Dillard made the call, you see, but I did take the column. Actually there wasn't anything really interesting in it! Kind of a pity after all that trouble—don't you think?"

"Why on earth did you put the envelope in my car?" Sudie said. "Was that supposed to make me look guilty?"

"Why, not at all, dear!" Miss Baby looked genuinely shocked. "I thought that was Jane's car. It was parked in her driveway overnight. After all, she had been asking a lot of questions, and she was the one who found Chloe's body.

"These old ropes really are hurting me," she said with a pleading look at Sudie. "Can't you just loosen them a little? If you'll let me go, I promise I won't try to get away."

I was ready with an appeal in her defense; a little speech about justice and mercy, and about how we would need Miss Baby's testimony to clear Nelson Fain. But I didn't have to give it. With a sigh Sudie leaned over and gave the ropes a tug: feet first, and then the hands. Immediately the teacher's bonds fell away, and I realized they hadn't even been knotted.

"Oh, go on!" Sudie said, giving the woman a little push. "I wasn't going to hurt you anyway!" She looked at me and shrugged. "I just wanted to give her a taste of her own medicine."

For a minute Miss Baby just stood in a state of confusion, looking from one to the other while she rubbed her wrists. Then, realizing she was free, she bolted from the clearing, stumbling and sliding through the underbrush along the way.

Someone laughed. It sounded strange, unfamiliar; I looked about. Who would be laughing at such a time? And then I knew: it was me. Our ordeal was finally over. I started for Sudie with a shout. Brave, loyal Sudie who had probably saved me from a fiery death and outwitted a cunning killer as well.

"Jane, no." Shagg grabbed my shirt and spun me around, shoving me to the ground, and I saw the whiff of smoke rise like a bad spirit from the forest floor. "Sudie, run!" he shouted. But it was too late. The ember from the second match had apparently smoldered in dry pine straw until it reached the ring of fuel. Now the circle ignited with a flash of red and blue, with Sudie screaming and helpless in the center!

Before I could get to my knees, Shagg broke off a green pine bough and beat a path through the flames; seconds later he reappeared with Sudie in his arms. "Hurry! This whole place is as dry as a tinder box! Nothing will stop it now!" With one of us on either side of him, he propelled us down the hillside and back the way we had come. "What about Miss Baby?" I said when we reached the place where we had left the car.

Sudie leaned over to breathe, holding her side. "I left her car on the side of the road down there." She shook her head. "She's probably in the next county by now."

"I don't think so." Shagg pointed to a convoy of vehicles approaching from the road. "Isn't that Miss Baby's car? Looks like a policeman at the wheel." He managed a soot-smeared smile. "The cavalry to the rescue!"

I glanced behind us at the bright glow on the hillside. I noticed the charred hem of Shagg's pants, the tiny black holes where embers had burned his sleeves, and I knew the heroes were already here. I turned and walked away from them to meet the first cars bumping across the field.

Chapter Twenty-five

Jericho had the door open on the passenger side of Papa Sam's car before it came to a full stop, and in the seconds it took to cover the space between us, I knew I was going to risk falling in love all over again.

After the second kiss someone behind us coughed. Not one to suffer in silence, Papa Sam took out a large white handkerchief and blew a loud blast. I threw my arms around him. "You're behind all this, aren't you? How long have you known?"

"Well, that depends . . ." He smelled like licorice cough drops and camphorated oil. "It was Baby Kennemore, wasn't it? Where is she?"

"Surely she's not still in those woods!" Sudie looked behind us. "She started out before we did."

One of the policemen got on the radio. "Don't worry; we'll find her. She won't go far!"

"Until recently I was sure it was Eulonia," my grandfather said as we drove back to town. "It was Dillard Moore's death that confused me. Now, she could have killed him if he found out about Aaron, but would she try to frame Jericho for the murder? That was an obvious setup—even the police didn't accept it!"

I snuggled closer to Jericho and closed my eyes. "You mean the hammer with his fingerprints?" I asked.

"Right. She could have taken the hammer, but it just didn't make sense . . . and I wasn't sure it was Baby Kennemore, either—not until today!"

Jericho's arm tightened around me. "The police called your grandfather after what happened this morning, and when we couldn't find you, we combed that whole area. Eulonia's house was still empty, and there was no one at Twin Towers, either; but we found a puddle of gasoline there under the storage room door."

"Still, Eulonia could've done that." I yawned.

"Not when she was in Washington," my grandfather said. "I thought that was where she'd gone, and when I called Aaron's sister out there this morning she told me Eulonia had parked herself on her living room sofa and showed no signs of leaving!" He laughed. "Well, by God, they're welcome to her!"

Later, he said, police turned up with a search warrant and found a tape in Dillard Moore's room telling all about the buried chemicals and the murders of Etta and Chloe. I guess he didn't trust his aunt any more than she trusted him.

"How did you know about Aaron Moody?" I asked.

"Eulonia bought her insurance from me, remember? And I'd seen this man's picture in her living room, so I knew who he was when I saw them together a few months ago. Even with the frizzy hair and sunglasses, he hadn't changed all that much."

The man had come by the drugstore to see Eulonia one day last fall when Papa Sam was there having lunch. "She couldn't get him out of the way fast enough!" he said. "Especially after she saw me there. Later I found some excuse to drop by her house and that picture had disappeared. And then, of course, there was Shelba Jean's new car. I knew stingy old Eulonia'd never turn loose of that kind of money!"

"And she really thought he was dead all those years?"

Jericho stroked my fingers. "Aaron Moody just took advantage of a serendipitous situation. Eulonia made him take out a large insurance policy because of his work, but he didn't plan to cash in on it. He was miserable in his marriage—and who could blame him? And when a vagrant was killed in the demolition of the old mill, Aaron switched identities. Eulonia and the child would have financial security, and Aaron Moody would have his freedom. The two men were about the same size and the tramp was burned beyond recognition. From that day on he became Elias Hawkins, and from what I've learned, he's done okay for himself out in the northwest." He smiled. "Shelba Jean had a more recent photograph of her father hidden behind that old beach snapshot she kept by her bed. That was what I took from her room."

"I wonder why he didn't just stay out there? Nobody would ever have known."

"Shelba Jean. Remember? He couldn't forget he was a father," Papa Sam reminded me. "I think he must have checked on the girl from time to time. And lately he didn't like what he was seeing. He tried to get her to come back with him to Washington, get some help for her problems, and when all else failed, he used the new car as a bribe." He smiled. "That must've been a hell of a shock to Eulonia having him suddenly come 'alive' after all that time."

"But what about Cousin Myra?" I asked Jericho. "She said they identified Eulonia's husband after that explosion. She sounded so *sincere.*"

"Cousin Myra was a plant," he explained. "You were asking too many questions and you would keep reminding her about the man on the motorcycle! Eulonia sent us there on purpose. The woman was paid to lie."

"Well, where is Shelba Jean? What happened to her?"

"Getting help, I hope," my grandfather said. "Her daddy checked her into some kind of rehabilitation center up in Washington state. He has kinfolks up there who'll look after her."

"And she's been there all this time?"

"Not by a long shot!" Papa Sam said. "Ran off with some beach bum after she made that promise to her daddy—tried to give old Aaron the slip!" He shook his head. "By the time I found them a couple of days later at some cheap motel off Ocean Drive, the bloom was off the romance already. I think that little girl was downright glad to see me."

"How did you know how to find her?" I asked.

"Letters. Eulonia found those letters she'd hidden, the ones from that lifeguard she'd run off with, and some of her friends said the two had made plans to meet. We had that much to go on."

"I'm surprised she agreed to let her go up there—to Washington, I mean."

"She didn't. Eulonia didn't know I was working with Aaron. And I did mean to tell her where Shelba Jean was as soon as she was under a professional's care, but then it looked like Eulonia might be up to her mustache in murder!"

I bolted upright as two fire trucks roared past, sirens screaming, on their way to the Widow's Woods. I looked behind us at the glowing orange mound. Thick, choking smoke hovered over the valley, and now and then ashes sifted down with the wind. I hoped it would burn to the ground taking all its meanness with it!

"Sudie said Miss Baby killed Dillard," I said as we pulled into our driveway. "Her own nephew. Why?"

"Greed, I suppose," my grandfather said. "I can't be sure, but it looks like Dillard tried to blackmail his aunt for a share of the profits from the woods sale. He knew about the PCB, you see, and the things she'd done to conceal it. She knew he was going out to that old church that day, so she followed him there and crushed his skull with her own hammer, planning to blame it on Jericho."

"Why Jericho?"

"He'd been seen with Dillard, she'd heard the two of them arguing, and he had disappeared without a word. Baby Kennemore thought he was just another one of her nephew's misplaced flock and, since he was Etta's uncle, a likely scapegoat for her scheme."

• • •

I had left the windows open and the smell of gasoline was almost gone from the house. I pulled Jericho's face down for a quick kiss as Papa Sam put on a pot of coffee. My eyelids felt as if they had weights on them, but I couldn't sleep—not yet. I watched Papa Sam measure coffee into the percolator and snap the lid into place. If I sat down I would fall asleep. "You and Jericho. You've known each other all along, haven't you? Don't you think it's time we were introduced?"

"Etta was my sister's only child," Jericho said. "It was bad enough for her to die the way she did, but we couldn't stand not knowing why—or who. I couldn't bear to watch my sister grieve herself to death and just do nothing, so I came here to see if I could find some answers. I didn't think anyone would know me here."

"But he forgot about me," Papa Sam said.

Jericho had worked briefly for an insurance associate of my grandfather's several years before while he was earning his graduate degree. Since the firm was in another town, the two usually talked over the phone, but on a couple of occasions the situation required a meeting. Then, only a few months ago, my grandfather had seen Jericho Scott with his family at Etta Lucas's funeral.

"When he confronted me this summer I had to admit it," Jericho said. "That's when we joined forces, so to speak."

"I was already suspicious about Aaron Moody," Papa Sam said. "You see, my insurance company was the one who paid off on that false claim. I've got stock in that company, and I sure as hell didn't like to see money going down the drain. Anyway, since he was living over at the Kennemores', I asked him to keep an eye on Eulonia as well. I had an idea Aaron Moody might turn up again." He glanced at Jericho. "And then, after Chloe was killed, it began to look like Eulonia had something to do with it." My grandfather got down mugs for the three of us. "I don't mind telling you, Jane, I was mighty glad he was there next door."

Papa Sam knew that Aaron only wanted to help his

daughter, so when Shelba Jean disappeared he faced him and made a deal. "I just bought him a little time," he said. "At first he claimed to be the girl's uncle, said her daddy's family sent him here. Hell, I knew very well who he was, but I knew I'd have to prove it, so I just played along with him."

When Papa Sam located Shelba Jean at the beach he immediately got in touch with her "uncle" and accompanied the two to Washington where Aaron made arrangements at the center.

I eyed the percolator, empty mug in my hand. The coffee smelled wonderful. "And you came back that same night Eulonia lured me to the woods?"

Papa Sam nodded. "Aaron and I flew back together. After what happened to Chloe, he didn't trust Eulonia either; and when he came back and found her gone that night, and when I couldn't get an answer from you, we suspected something was wrong. Cooter had gone home, you see, thinking you were safe in bed upstairs, and of course I had no way of knowing Jericho would be watching over the Satan worshippers from within the cult."

I sipped the steaming coffee and propped my chin in my hand. "So that *was* Aaron Moody who scared the cultists away?"

"After we called the police." Papa Sam ladled jam on toast. "Man rides like a hornet on that thing. He was the one who fixed your car, too, Jane. I think Eulonia did that to add to your hysterical image as much as anything else."

"Remind me to thank him," I said. "Where is he, by the way?"

"Aaron turned himself in for insurance fraud last night," Jericho said, holding his coffee mug up for more. He smiled at me. "Black as the devil, hot as hell, pure as an angel, sweet as love," he said.

I felt my eyelids closing in spite of the caffeine. "What?"

"Old recipe for coffee." His voice seemed to come from far away.

I looked at him through little puffy-eyed slits. "Tell me —what do you do the rest of the year?"

He pulled my head onto his shoulder and kissed the top of my head. "I'm a professor. I teach—"

"No, don't tell me! Let me guess. English. You teach English and literature."

"How did you know?"

I laughed. "Lucky guess."

While Papa Sam called the police station to ask if they'd found Miss Baby I stretched out on the back porch hammock. Jericho pulled a chair close and reached for my hand. "Why didn't you tell somebody what was going on?" I asked.

"Because we had no proof. That was my department. At first I thought Dillard had killed Etta. Then it looked as if Nelson Fain had murdered Chloe. And even after we learned who Elias Hawkins really was, we weren't absolutely sure about Eulonia's part in all of this." His hand circled my arm and stayed there. "And we almost waited too late."

"What about the Satan worshippers?" I asked.

"A bad news lot," Jericho said. "Etta was involved I'm afraid; Shelba Jean, too. They were into drugs in a big way. My sister would never believe it, but I found that out when I went to a couple of those meetings. Eulonia guessed, I think, what was happening to her daughter, but she just couldn't handle it. Miss Baby knew, of course, and she used what she knew of those symbols to mislead the police, make them think the first two deaths were a result of some kind of black magic."

"Maybe they were." I looked into the morning sun and felt it warm on my face. I had never seen such sun! It shone through the dark residue of the fire, washing the whole yard in a yellow light. Now maybe the light could touch us all.

Shagg would probably lose his job, but he was going to be all right, I thought, after he learned to deal with his feelings of guilt over Etta's death. He had reminded me of the old Shagg as he left to drive Sudie from the woods to the police station where Nelson would soon be released.

"What about Aaron Moody?" I asked. "Will he have to serve time?"

"Maybe not," Jericho said. "At least he should get off with a light sentence, since he promised to pay back with interest the amount Eulonia had collected from the insurance company."

I looked up to see my grandfather standing in the doorway with a strained look on his face. "Baby Kennemore never made it out of the woods," he said.

"But she left before the fire started! She must have gotten out."

Papa Sam shook his head. "Looks like she slipped and hit her head; some of those hills are steep. By the time they got to her it was too late."

The woods had claimed another victim. I hoped it would be the last.

I closed my eyes. I had listened to Papa Sam's stories too often. The Widow Brumley was only a fairy tale—a Hansel and Gretel fable. I had taken a harmless old woman, long dead, and woven her into an apparition of supernatural horror. There was no evil Widow Brumley.

I looked up to see Jericho watching over me. "The night of the widow's visit," I said sleepily, "Shagg said it wasn't Eulonia. It must have been Miss Baby! But I wonder how she got inside. And those eyes, those awful yellow eyes. How did she do that?"

Jericho squeezed my fingers. "I'm afraid that's one thing you can't blame on your neighbor—as rotten as she was. I saw Miss Baby's light come on as soon as you screamed, and I watched her as she came scurrying from Twin Towers like a little gray spider to see what was going on." He kissed my hand. "It was a nightmare, Jane. You had a bad dream."

But I knew otherwise. I had said nothing to the others, but I was sure I had heard an old woman's mocking laughter when Sudie was surrounded with fire in that dark place where the devil whispers behind the leaves. I had seen the widow herself.